DANGER: HIGH VOLTAGE

I spun quickly with the razor and slashed Big Head from his shoulder to the opposite hip. It wasn't a deep cut, but it caused enough pain to drive him backward and into a stunned silence as he stared at the red streak across his shirt.

I had allowed Logger too much time to react, my attention fixed on Big Head. A blinding pulse of direct current zapped through me as Logger stabbed me with the twin copper jaws of the jumper cable. Every muscle in my body spasmed.

Clasping the rubber insulators, he leaned his weight fully into me. My vision went red, and then there was nothing. . . .

Also by Wendell McCall:

Dead Aim

Wendell McCall

AIM

FOR THE

HEART

A Chris Klick Mystery

A DELL BOOK

Published by
Dell Publishing
a division of
Bantam Doubleday Dell Publishing Group, Inc.
666 Fifth Avenue
New York, New York 10103

This book is a work of fiction. All of the events, characters, and
places depicted in this novel are entirely fictitious or are used
fictitiously. No representation that any statement made in this
novel is true or that any incident depicted in this novel actually
occurred is intended or should be inferred by the reader.

ISBN: 0-440-21082-8

Reprinted by arrangement with St. Martin's Press, New York,
New York

Printed in the United States of America

Published simultaneously in Canada

November 1991

10 9 8 7 6 5 4 3 2 1

RAD

Dedicated to those who live in the flight path . . .

1

There is nothing quite as satisfying as a morning run. There are things more enjoyable, but nothing quite as satisfying. In the mountains, at that moment in time when the sun is about to crest the eastern ridge, rays splintering into a sky littered with clouds, the air becomes absolutely still, as if the earth is holding its breath, awaiting the new day.

Padding along the rutted dirt road that curled around a sage-covered hill below Tom and Julie Shanklin's A-frame, I was greeted with the first trumpeting of a robin, a welcome burst of melody interrupting the stillness. Within moments neighboring birds joined in, and soon a whistled chorus charged the dawn with an intoxicating energy.

My friend Lyel's new puppy, Derby, trotted at my side, her tail wagging, tongue drooping. Part shepherd, part collie, with sad brown eyes and a coy, baby-toothed grin, she was a joyful companion.

I have never been accused of being a workaholic. I spend as much time as possible in appreciation of life and the world around me. For this reason, I have not accumulated enough capital reserve to acquire any material goods of significant permanence. No house. No property. No stocks or bonds or securities of any sort. I divide my time between work and play as unequally as possible. Work is tied loosely to the edges of the music business and a partner in L.A. The reason I had been able to take time off to play was that I had spent the month of May locating a woman who had once been a member of a popular Motown trio. I had found her in Baltimore, where she and her husband ran a motel, and across town, a coin-op laundry. She was due a generous amount of money that my partner, Bruce Warren, had pried loose from a record company. The money, back royalties, had been buried for years in the tabular columns of a ledger book. For our part, Bruce and I split twenty-five percent of the pretax amount, which came to $18,500. I had left Los Angeles with a little shy of nine grand, a sum I hoped might carry me through a summer of fly-fishing and birding in the dusty hills of central Idaho.

I turned around at the third gate up Townsend Gulch, a distance that made my round trip run just over four miles. As I passed the Shanklins' again, I noticed the Dobermans were out and roaming, so I kept Derby close. She was still of a size and naiveté that would make her little more than a breakfast muffin for a Doberman, even though the Shanklins' Dobermans are as gentle as lambs. She growled and whined, tucking her previously wagging tail submissively between her scurrying legs as she strode alongside, one eye cocked toward her adversaries, who had the consideration to halt at the big gate and allow us to pass.

A mile and a half later the two of us turned right onto the narrow gravel lane that feeds Lyel's property, property I have come to think of as my own. Lyel allows me residence in the "guest cottage," a log cabin that sits alongside a deliciously private trout stream that plays host to an enormous amount of bird life. He occupies the main house, seven thousand square feet of bachelor opulence, if and when he's in town, which amounts to about the same span of time that I'm in town. Therein lies the absurdity of the designation "house sitter," a title he once bestowed upon me. Lyel *always* arrives in town shortly after I do, and *always* stays until I leave. In short, he could just as easily house sit, since he's there when I'm there.

* * *

Lyel showed up just before noon as I was contemplating the enormous task before me: installing a lawn sprinkling system. Lyel had ordered the parts; I was supposed to supply the labor. He had brought me a St. Pauli Girl and a turkey sandwich from the Southside Deli in Butte Peak. We left Derby sleeping in the shade of the deck and took a break beneath the dancing leaves of a mountain ash. Lyel wore red and black jams, a white cotton golf shirt, and size fourteen flip-flops. I asked him where he found flip-flops that size and he told me that they had been hanging as demonstration models in the local drugstore.

Lyel keeps himself young by surrounding himself with young women. He has two housecleaners, a woman to mow his lawn, and a part-time cook. All four look perfectly wonderful in bikinis, and all seem to appreciate Lyel as much as I do—though in a different way.

A distant sound caught his attention. "Ag-cat," Lyel said. He knows airplanes the way I know birds. The small plane was flying low, traveling from our right, passing directly over the town of Ridland and headed for a landing at Butte Peak's small regional airport.

"Um," I acknowledged in mid bite. Small planes don't do much for me, except interrupt my serenity and scare away birds.

It wasn't until the plane exploded that I paid any attention; and then, because it was several miles away,

it seemed somewhat surreal. A huge yellow-orange
mushroom erupted into the tranquil blue of that mid-
day sky, driving a black cloud of smoke above it like a
top hat.

A moment later a second explosion rocked the
ground beneath us. We were four miles away, and we
glanced at each other in disbelief. A tower of red-black
flame peaked at about a hundred feet.

"That," Lyel said, "was the gas station."

Lyel was seldom wrong.

2

I have never been attracted to accidents. The sight of blood, especially human blood, makes me ill, though for some reason I have seen more than my share of it. I wasn't in Lyel's car barreling toward the flames from any love of accidents, I was in his car because the two of us, being large in stature and strong of build, have helped out the volunteer fire crew a number of times, and there was no doubt they would need our help today. Steven Garman, ski patrolman, private pilot, fireman, and friend, had solicited our help some years back when a nearby barn went up in flames, threatening the lives of several valuable Arabian horses locked in stalls inside. The horses lived. From that day forward, Lyel and I had been considered auxiliary firemen.

As we came up the highway, we noticed traffic had already been detoured toward the high school. A number of drivers had pulled off the road to watch the blaze and the efforts to bring it under control. Lyel made the turn toward the high school, away from the spectacular flames, and parked in the lot of a real estate office. Sheriff Dan Norton, who was keeping the crowd of onlookers back, let us through. Lyel knew Norton well. Lyel knows everyone well.

Steven, clad in a fireman's rubber suit, was red in the

face. He spotted us and hurried over. "Thank God," he said. "We need every hand we can get. Whole damn station went up."

What was left of the plane was standing on its nose and flaming like a gigantic wick. It had made a gaping hole in the chain-link fence that surrounded the airport.

"How about the pilot?" I asked.

"He bit it," Steven informed us. "Looks like he tried to jump as he approached the fence. Might have made it too, but he landed on an old pipe sticking out of the ground."

"Jump?" I asked. But Steven was already turning back to the blaze.

"Extra suits on the truck, guys. Not that they'll fit you."

I saw another plume of smoke rising at our right.

"Mark's place!" I hollered, pointing. Then another finger of flame went up on the left. "The rodeo arena."

"Damn," Steven shouted, cupping his hands over his eyes to study the rooftops of the buildings in the immediate area. "Fallout from the two explosions," he said. The burning debris, returning to earth, had ignited these and probably other structures.

Lyel is such a huge man that his voice commands authority. When he said, "We'll take Mark's," there was no argument from Steven.

"There's a plug on the corner of that block," Steven said. "Take a hose and a wrench."

We grabbed the thick rubber suits and the hose and wrench from the ladder truck, piled everything into Lyel's Wagoneer, and raced the two blocks to Mark Acker's Snow Lake Animal Clinic. It was far worse than I'd expected. What had been a tiny tendril of smoke only minutes before had developed quickly into a raging blaze. Most of the roof was afire. Worse yet, there was no sign of Mark or Nancy, his assistant.

Even as only occasional volunteers, Lyel and I were

well practiced; we were into the gear and had the hose
hooked up and running within minutes. A running fire
hose is nothing to fool around with; fortunately, both
Lyel and I can hold our own against the bucking force.
We adopted the stance, legs spread to lower our centers
of gravity, arms hugging the canvas hose, Lyel on the
nozzle, me just behind him. We arced the spray high
into the air; it fell on the edge of the burning hole in the
roof. Clouds of steam mixed with the smoke and flame.
To the untrained eye the fire appeared suddenly much
worse.

"Too little too late," I yelled at him over the roar of
water and flame. I watched his huge helmeted head
nod. We both looked silly in our black fire hats, but rules
were rules. I was roasting in the thick rubber suit.
"We're going to lose all the animals if we don't do something."

"Where the hell is Mark?" Lyel shouted back at me.

Clearly, if we waited much longer we would lose our
chance to enter the building. "We're not going to get
any backup," I roared. "It's now or never."

"Agreed," he returned, the anxiety plain in his voice.

"So which is it?" I asked.

"Now," he said, indicating with a jerk of his head that
I should kill the water. I left him to battle the strength of
the hose and twisted the huge nut on top of the fireplug.

Entering a burning building is as close as any of us get
to a look inside hell. Not only do heat and flame sur-
round you, but the combustion consumes most of the
available oxygen, leaving an unmasked fire fighter gasping for breathable air.

The front door was unlocked, but with smoke visible
through the windows, we knew better than to throw the
door open and charge inside. The starved fire would
feed off the fresh air and probably blow us to kingdom
come. We each picked up one of the large river rocks
that bordered the parking lot of the one-story animal

clinic tossing them through the windows. As the glass broke, the gray smoke inside the reception area flashed yellow, then blue, and various areas of the room burst instantly into flame. The windows seemed to implode. Lyel and I rushed to the front door; I turned the handle and we stepped back and kicked it in. Another *whoosh* of flame raced from the door toward the smoke-filled hallway. I used combat hand signals to indicate I would take the back and that Lyel was to search the examination rooms straight ahead and the apartment wing to our right. He tried to wave me off, to switch assignments—the back was burning out of control. The barking and cries of caged animals frightening—but I didn't stick around to debate.

A huge piece of a gas pump had apparently crashed through the roof like a bomb, taking out the file room and a piece of the hall. I ducked and dodged around a burning beam. The last I saw of Lyel was as he carefully opened the door to the first examination room.

Beyond the fallen beam the hallway grew thick with smoke, the agony of the trapped animals deafening. I was immediately tempted to check the two other examination rooms to my left, but fighting fire is like fighting a battle: once the assignments are made, they must be adhered to. Systematic teamwork is the key to success, and it is in this area that Lyel and I excel. Over the past few years we had found ourselves in our fair share of difficult situations—more than our fair share. We were something like war buddies in this regard, having learned how the other man responded to a given predicament, what to expect, what to avoid. I knew better than to double-cover Lyel's assignment, especially with gut-wrenching screams coming from the other side of the far door.

I paused by the door, turning my head in case the flames shot out at me, and cracked it open. The acceleration of air was so intense that the door whistled, the tone descending the scale as the crack widened. My eyes stung from the thick, acrid smoke. I coughed, tasting charcoal. The patient ward: a cement floor I could feel but not see; chain-link cages, some floor-to-ceiling, some divided into small animal high-rises. The smoke was coming from the ceiling, and I knew from past experience that there is an ignition point to such smoke. The hole in the roof grows with the fire; the smoke collects in the "attic" area formed by the roof trusses. At some point the hole enlarges, the trapped smoke ignites, and the roof blows off. The tighter the house, the more chance of explosion into the rooms below. If the ceilings of those rooms catch fire, as had happened here, then the air comes in from the bottom and accelerates the process. My instinct told me to get out—this room had reached its flash point. Soon the dense cloud of smoke would spontaneously convert to flame.

The cacophony of the thirty house pets all crying at once at the top of their voices kept my adrenaline high. I blocked my instinct to run.

The latches on the cages were difficult to work with my gloved fingers. Door after door came open. Animals leapt out at me, bit at me, barked at me. By the time I reached the next to last pen, I had an army of quadrupeds at my feet.

If several of the dogs had not blown past me into the pen, I might have missed her. In an effort to shoo them back out into the team, I stepped on Nancy's leg. I knelt beside her. There was blood on her face, and she was unconscious. I gathered Nancy into my arms and rose, stumbling on the pets underfoot, and kicked open the latch on the last pen, freeing a certified criminal dog. It was a monster breed, with a front paw wrapped in white gauze and plaster. There was no hesitation whatsoever. He came after me with a vengeance, sinking his jaw into my rubber leggings and breaking the skin beneath. I tried to shake him off and nearly fell yet an-

other time; finally I turned and kicked his bad paw. He
whined in pain and backed off. I had reached the back
door; luckily, something inside me, a sense of self-pres-
ervation, alerted me to the fact that the moment I
opened this door, the gases in the room would ignite,
fueled by the fresh air. I hesitated.

Unluckily, in that moment of hesitation, the smoke
ignited, flames tearing across the ceiling. What spared
us was that the room contained nothing flammable. Fire
is like water: water seeks the lowest level; fire seeks air
and fuel. The smoke was fuel, and it burned off in a
single devastating flash of ignition, but the fire itself
ripped up into the overhead rafters toward the air, not
down toward me and my group. The dogs ran for the
door through which I had entered. I followed them
back out into the hallway, where I encountered Lyel,
who was just about to duck under the flaming beam. He
was tripped by the dogs and fell to his knees.

"I got Mark," he yelled, opening his arms so that I
might pass Nancy under the beam to him. He took her
and turned for the front door. I ducked under the beam
and grabbed Lyel's hips, pushing him forward more
quickly than he intended to move. Lyel has this thing
about not rushing in a crisis. It was time to rush.

We knew better than to rest at the first taste of fresh
air. I was coughing to beat hell, my lungs felt blistered.
But we ran. Once clear of the building, Lyel carried
Nancy effortlessly. I couldn't see Mark, but I figured
Lyel had put him in the Wagoneer. What a strange
sensation it was, to be running as fast as possible,
dragged into slow motion by the heavy rubber clothing.
Only then did I see that several of the dogs had no hair;
it had been singed off.

The explosion threw us to the ground. All of the available fuel in the building—wood, plastics, chemicals—
ignited at once into a single rolling curl of fire that shot
ferociously into the sky. The roof collapsed in an ear-

shattering finale. The walls folded in. In all, we had been inside three minutes. It had nearly been a lifetime.

We drove Mark and Nancy to the county hospital, not far from the fire. The doctor insisted on looking us over as well. He sent me on my way with an inhaler. By the time we returned, Steven had the two major fires, the gas station and the rodeo grounds, under control. We were told to go home. I noticed a pair of paramedics pulling the pilot off the vertical steel stake he had had the misfortune to dive onto. I tapped Lyel on the shoulder and pointed it out to him.

"Disgusting," he said.

"Why would he jump?" I asked.

"Wouldn't you have?"

I shrugged. I wanted to agree, but I couldn't see myself having the foresight to undo my seat belt, clear myself, open the door, and leap from a plane moving at fifty miles an hour, careening out of control down a runway. "This'll do great things for the airport's PR," I said. This airport, growing in leaps and bounds, was the target of much public outcry. The quiet mountain community of Butte Peak had become the destination point of commercial airlines, the new traffic shattering the peaceful existence expected of such a place. The airport continued to be the hot news in the local paper. Political careers were in jeopardy. This accident was certain to add to the controversy.

I headed over to the paramedics. Lyel elected not to follow.

They were about to place the pilot in a body bag. The man had a messy chest. My stomach turned. His face was quiet and peaceful. One of the paramedics noticed me. "Tough luck," I said.

"Damn tough luck," the paramedic agreed. "He had it timed damn near perfectly, by the look of it. Shit, the runway ends and the highway is right there. He's got what, forty feet of grass to hit? He should have lived. Shitty break."

The man's shirt was torn open, and I noticed he was wearing an undershirt. It was a warm time of year to be wearing undershirts, even at fifteen thousand feet. A couple of pieces of shiny fabric were lying in the grass by the bloody stake. They were soiled, but I couldn't help myself. I squatted down and fingered one. Unusual material.

The paramedic saw me. "No souvenirs. Norton'll want all that shit for the investigation. FAA will be in on this. Better not touch anything." I nodded, my eyes fixed on the long straight stretch of black tarmac reaching south. Heat caused a mirage of water on its surface. The blue landing lights were kept illuminated even during the day. A small red-and-white-painted building caught my attention. It was new, and I recognized it as the Microwave Landing System that had been at the center of the public controversy for the past few months. Now that it was on line, planes could instrument-land in inclement weather. I was aware of it because the system demanded an approach pattern over the town of Butte Peak, rather than from the south. It was a change Lyel and I had welcomed: the old approach pattern went over Lyel's property. The air traffic had increased steadily in the last few years, and this change in direction due to the MLS meant less noise for us, but more for the residents of Butte Peak. This was the residents' major complaint. Concern over possible pilot error ranked right up there. "You hear me?" the paramedic asked.

I put the fabric down and rose. "Right," I said, wondering why the plane had landed from the south. So many used the approach from the north these days. Probably something to do with good weather and wind patterns.

"You coming?" Lyel hollered from a distance.

I nodded and joined him. We left our gear on the fire truck and walked back to Lyel's Jeep Wagoneer.

"They're lucky," he said. "Only one man dead, from what I hear. The pilot."

"What about whoever was in there?" I asked, pointing to the charred gas station.

Lyel shook his head. "That's what I mean by lucky. Place was closed because of road repair. This stretch of road is closed what, once every two years for repair? If that."

"That's a nice coincidence," I said.

"Don't start with me, Klick. Luck is luck, that's what it is. Some of us have it, some of us don't. You and I, we get our share."

I've never been fond of coincidence. I'm more from the everything-happens-for-a-reason school.

We were driving back toward home, alongside the runway and the perimeter fence. A long time ago this town had been a good place for a private airport, but that was before the excessive commercial development of the Snow Lake resort, which shared the airport. It had grown into one of the busiest airports in the state, second only to the one serving the capital, Boise, and the added air traffic presented risks to the public. An accident like this one proved the complaints were well founded. Furthermore, the noise pollution detracted from a quality of life, which was the very reason people moved to the area. To make matters worse, commercialization was limited. The small runways were impossible to expand due to the availability of land, which restricted the size of aircraft that could land and made Snow Lake more difficult to reach than any other western resort. With the rapid growth of ski areas around Salt Lake City and the expansion of both Idaho's and Colorado's ski areas, Snow Lake had become less attractive to the vacation skier, and the economic fallout had been heavy in the past few years. The arguments were all there for relocating the airport to an area that would allow expansion. Relocation would make it possible for larger jets to land, which would mean direct flights from major cities by major carriers.

Despite all of this, the mayor of Butte Peak, who also happened to be the manager of the airport, ignored such arguments. The big money businesses of Snow Lake opposed relocation, favoring expansion of the existing airport despite the complaints of locals, because a new airport would further distance the resort town from a quick-commute airport transportation hub. The bus ride between the airport and Snow Lake took thirty minutes in bad weather, and the chamber of commerce didn't want this to increase. It was an issue that deeply divided the valley.

As we drove past the end of the runway, I spotted a group of workers frantically spraying water on one of the hayfields belonging to the Flying Heart Ranch. Nearly a mile from the burned gas station, it confirmed the potential danger of a large fire in an area considered high desert.

"The thing is," I said to Lyel, who I knew didn't want to hear anything about it, "I don't see how the pilot could have reacted so quickly. I mean, think about it. Right now, even in these seats, say we're doing seventy-five or eighty, and what, twenty yards ahead is a stopped truck. Now you realize the brakes don't work. Hand brake doesn't work. You have to unfasten the seat belt, open the door, and jump." I unfastened my seat belt and yanked on the handle.

"Klick!" he shouted, wondering if I was mad enough to try it.

I looked back at a road marker. "We're doing what, sixty? And it took me three markers to do all that. Nearly a third of a mile. You see?" He grumbled in annoyance. I refastened my seat belt and sat placidly, a good little boy. "The guy had brass balls," I said, finally.

"He was headed for a fence, Klick. You might have jumped, too."

"You're missing my point."

"Which is?"

"He didn't have time to think about jumping. He would have to have been planning the jump well before he landed."

"Did it ever occur to you he might have known he was in trouble? Maybe an instrument light came on or something. Maybe he knew in advance." I could tell from his tone of voice that his impatience with me had hit critical mass.

"Maybe," I said. But I didn't believe it. I'm not fond of easy explanations, especially where dead bodies are concerned.

3

The next day I returned from my morning run to find a shirtless Bill Pereira sitting on my front lawn. His Thermos bottle was filled with steaming coffee. His dirt-crusted right fist held a bran muffin. A landscaper, Bill possesses the upper body of a weightlifter, barrel-chested and with arms of pure brawn. A smile appeared on his pleasantly boyish face. The Ditch Witch, an enormous motor-driven digger, sat idle on the far side of the lawn, where one of Bill's workers was enjoying a cigarette. "Hey, buddy," he said jovially.

"Lyel will be pleased," I said. Bill's crew had been scheduled to begin work a few days earlier.

"They fixed up the Ditch Bitch. Some jerk had broken the recoil." He slurped at the coffee. "Lyel says you're going to do most of the work yourself."

"Lucky me."

Lyel had suggested that the new sprinkler system would make life easier and had asked me if I would provide the labor if he covered the cost. I find working with my hands extremely satisfying, though I'm not particularly skilled in this department. Nothing quite like the feeling of accomplishment from a job well done. I accepted his invitation. The idea made me giddy: in a few short days I would be able to throw a switch and all of the lawn surrounding Lyel's guest cabin would be watered automatically. As it was, I had been spending many hours a day moving hose around the place.

Bill and his boys left me with over a thousand feet of three-inch-wide ditch, an equal length of a combination of PVC pipe sizes, a huge cardboard box containing a hundred different elbows, Ts, and sprinklers, and enough insecurity to make Derby seem arrogant. His wounded truck lumbered down my private lane, swallowed by a self-generated ball of gray dust.

I put on plastic gloves, grabbed my hacksaw, and prepared to begin gluing miles of pipe together. I had to wonder about Lyel's true purpose for the project. Did he really need the sprinkler system, or was he just trying to keep me busy? I knew he was worried about me; he had said as much a few weeks earlier. I had been whining lately, and this he reminded me of at every opportunity. Actually, pining was more like it. Pining for a woman named Nicole, hoping she might return to fill the aching void she had left me with. If this was love, then it hurt. I feared it was. Nicole changed my mood. Around her I felt different, I acted different. What made matters worse, I hardly knew her. How could I love her? I had helped her out of some trouble; we had enjoyed each other. She had left. Abruptly. Quite possibly permanently. And so I whined.

Since Nicole, I had filled my time with St. Pauli Girls, and three different job assignments—two strikeouts and then the woman in Baltimore. Now here I was back in Ridland, with its gentle mornings, hot afternoons, and cool mountain evenings. I knew expectation had no place in my life. Expectation is a form of mental cancer. Nonetheless, I found myself expecting Nicole's voice each time the phone rang, expecting to see her shining face when I heard the driveway growl beneath tires.

Since I was home and outside, I had not activated any of the modest security devices that we had built into the

guest cabin, so when Lyel drove up he took me by
surprise. I was, at that moment on a break, taking in the
colorful beauty of a male lazuli bunting, his brilliant
blue hood, the sharp stroke of black on his wing, and the
waistcoat of white. A group of about six pair of lazuli
alternately shared the feeder outside the kitchen's bay
window. I hadn't seen any hummingbirds for weeks on
the adjacent feeder, and I wondered if the lazuli were
scaring them off.

With Lyel's arrival, the lazuli flew away. I watched
the bird closely until it disappeared into the hedge of
Geyer's willows that line the spring-fed creek—the
slough—which borders the property.

"May I?" Lyel asked, coming out onto the deck from
inside the house, a beer in hand and an inquiring expression on his face. He dragged a deck chair over and
sat, stretching out his legs and sliding down in the chair.
He and I are both too big to look right in any chair.

"To what do I owe this pleasure?" I asked.

"You're not going to like it."

Lyel and I speak a kind of private shorthand. We often
interrupt each other in mid sentence because no further communication is required. But this was one of
those times I could not read him, and I decided to wait
him out, which is the way one deals with Lyel. The
lazuli returned, daring, confident, yet wary. Still no
hummingbirds.

"You came here to take a vacation. Am I right?" he
asked.

"You're right: I'm not liking this already."

"How long this time?"

"If you need the guesthouse, just say. I'll go backpack-
ing or something. I'd really like to get out in the back
country this summer, anyway. It's no skin off my neck."

"It's not that, Klick."

"I'm staying through August, if the money holds out
and if I'm not called out on a job."

"Is Bruce working on something?"

"He's always working on something. He claims this one is going to be a biggie. He implied it would take most of the summer to sort out. He takes the record company to court in late July. He vacations a few weeks in August, so I think I'm in the clear. Why the curiosity?"

"So you have plenty of time to unwind," he stated.

"Why the sales pitch? Don't move," I hissed. A black-chinned hummingbird buzzed up to the feeder and sampled the offering. She chattered loudly and flew away.

"It needs cleaning," Lyel suggested.

If there's one thing that really bothers me, it's people telling me how to deal with my birds. Lyel was well aware of this.

"I cleaned it," I insisted.

"Just a suggestion."

"It's too close to the seed feeder," I informed him.

"Maybe," he said, tilting the green bottle and chugging down some beer. It was clear that he didn't buy my explanation.

"Why the soft sell?" I reiterated.

"I've had a strange request. Strange, in that it was difficult to say no to. Mind you, all I agreed to do was to ask."

"Ask *me*?"

"Yes. The thing is," he said apologetically, "there are some people I just plain feel sorry for, especially people with no place to turn."

"What exactly are we talking about here?"

"And since you clearly have a Robin Hood streak in you—"

"Lyel."

He looked out toward the slough. Another humming-bird, a rufous male this time, approached from the willows, flying low, and stopped abruptly at the feeder. He rejected it as well. "Maybe it needs more sugar," I suggested.

"I ran into her at the grocery store. She's sort of a friend of a friend," he added.

"Her?"

I looked over at him, wondering where this might lead. We were both silent for a moment. There are times when I gaze into the proverbial mirror and see a perfectly acceptable fellow; at other times I see *him*, the one who resists growing up, who shuns responsibility, the one who volunteers none of his free time, who drinks expensive beer in the late afternoon sun and considers no one's problems but his own. I hate *him*.

Yet another rufous hummingbird gave it a go and then got up and went. This repetition was depressing me. I stood, grabbed Lyel's empty beer bottle, snatched the hummingbird feeder from its nail, and carried everything inside. I rinsed out the beer bottles and put them in the pile back by the washer-dryer for recycling. Then I washed the feeder—again, this time thoroughly —and refilled it with a mixture I kept in the refrigerator for just this purpose. I hung it back up and went to fetch two cold beers from the garage fridge. By the time I sat down, a black-chinned hummingbird was hovering happily by the feeder, his bill locked at the source. Lyel gloated. "Cleaned it, didn't you?" When I failed to answer he said, "Her sister is missing. She read about you in the paper—about us, actually—and asked if you ever did things for free."

"Do I?" I inquired with a suspicious glance.

"I told her I would ask."

"No, Lyel. You told her more than that."

"I told her you were a wonderful man, a dear friend, and that I would do what I could."

"Does she have a name?"

"Candice," he said.

"Ah, she's coming alive."

"*She's* very much alive, I assure you. She isn't so sure about her sister Roberta."

* * *

Candy was indeed very much alive, and that was how she introduced herself, as Candy, not Candice. She was about twenty-three, with sparkling green eyes, an alluring smile, and yet a country-girl shyness. Her sun-baked skin glowed, and she had that certain look of a woman overworked and tired. We sat down at a small table covered with a well-used oilcloth. At this early hour, we owned the Southside Deli.

I am a sucker for a woman in distress. It has gotten me into trouble more times than I can count. I was born with the curse of not knowing how to say no. Lyel looked over at me and grinned. It was a shit-eating grin that said *I knew you'd say yes.* All I had said so far was hello.

"Bert and I work over at the county courthouse, Mr. Klick," Candy began. "She works in records; I work in P and Z, planning and zoning. Second floor. Good jobs. We don't live together, but we see each other every day.

"She lives in Sage Hill, you know, over to the tennis club. Been two days now, and I ain't seen nor heard from her." Her eyes darted between Lyel and me. Some women might try this as a ploy; Candy McGreggor seemed genuinely afraid. "I called Nick. That's her man. He works at the garage. A mechanic, you know. He ain't seen her neither. I told Sheriff Norton about it, but he says there ain't nothing nobody can do about it, 'cept put her name on a wire or something. I seen Lyel yesterday, and he says he knows you pretty good, and so I asked him if there ain't something you can do to help me out. Swear to God, if I had the money I would pay you. But I just bought me a new car, and with the payments and all, I don't have nothing left over."

Hearing her speak made my heart sink. I had had similar experiences: I would spot a beautiful woman, apparently single, and fall immediately in love, only to have her open her mouth and ruin everything by speaking in a thick, unflattering accent. Or by chewing gum. Or both. Of course, if you live wherever the accent is from, she's still beautiful. Or if you happen to like gum.

I asked Candy, "Any ideas? Anything at all?"

"I've made a zillion calls. No one has seen her."

"When was the last time anyone saw her?"

"When she left work Monday. Four-thirty we get off. She didn't show for work the next morning. I checked with Nick, and he says he ain't seen her neither." Her face tightened. I noticed her misuse of eye shadow. It made her eyelids look like window shades.

"I'll poke around," I told her.

Lyel relaxed noticeably. Candy blinked through cloudy eyes and said, "Really?"

"No charge," I added, wondering why I always make such a big deal about money. Money seems to control my life, and I resent it.

"I'll pay you," she insisted. "Not to worry." Lyel glared at me. "It'll just have to be on time, that's all. Soon as I pay off the car—"

"No need to," I interrupted. "Let me just poke around some and see what I can come up with first."

She nodded enthusiastically. "I appreciate it, Mr. Klick. Hey, I could clean your house. Something like that. Maybe we could work a trade until I'm back in the cash. Whattaya say?"

Unlike white-collar Snow Lake, a full half of the economy of the lower valley revolves around barter. Instead of paying each other for services or products, people trade. No cash, no receipt means no taxes, no Uncle Sam, no panic over payment. A farmer trades an electrician two tons of hay in exchange for repair of a blown circuit in the barn. A restaurant trades a carpenter meal credit for some handiwork. Around and around it goes, as it has for thousands of years.

I would have insulted her by refusing the offer. The people of Ridland and Butte Peak are not without their pride. "We'll work something out," I assured her.

"I'm a damn good housecleaner. Really. How about this Saturday?"

"We'll see."

"Let's count on this Saturday, then. About ten o'clock?"

"We'll see," I said.

She held out her hand and I shook it. She gripped my hand strongly and looked me right in the eye. It's the Candys of this world that keep the Avon reps going. "Deal," she said. "And thanks a lot."

* * *

"Lyel," I complained as I climbed into his Wagoneer. "That was extremely unfair."

"She's a good kid. Besides, sitting around isn't helping you any."

"I'm not sitting around," I complained, "I'm installing your sprinkler system."

"*My* system? And just who does it benefit, may I ask?"

"I'm supposed to be on *vacation*. Finding missing people is my *work*."

"Which only underlines the fact that you're the right man for the job."

I looked over at him. I was tongue-tied.

"Good," he said. "That's over with. Now, where do we start?"

"*We?*"

"I am volunteering my time."

"You must like this kind of work."

"It's awesome," he said, purposely sounding like a teenager.

"Rad," I said.

"That too."

We were traveling down Broadmore Road, an old twisting road that follows the river and has little traffic because of the faster two-lane highway that runs down the center of the valley. It is said that there had once been a town called Broadmore, some five thousand strong, mostly Chinese, that sprang up in the late 1800s around the Twisted Gorge mine. There isn't a shred of physical evidence remaining. Nothing left of Broadmore, except for several hundred thousand cubic yards of mine tailings. Even a hundred years later, the mine tailings are so chemically out of balance that nothing will grow where they lie.

Not a single home site can be found. No roads. There are plenty of ways to explain the disappearance of Broadmore, what with the floods and fires the valley has seen over the last hundred years. Still, without a single board found decaying in a field, without a single rutted wagon wheel path, I remain skeptical that Broadmore ever existed.

I was also skeptical that Candy's sister was in any kind of trouble. A young woman fleeing the confines of the small town was not exactly headline material.

I asked Lyel to stop the car at the bridge. He shut off the engine and we got out. Leaning against the cement retaining walls, we listened to the churning river below. I recognized the call of a great horned owl coming from the woods, and in the distance the growl of a small plane. "What kind?" I asked him.

"Single engine. Skyhawk maybe."

"We live in a beautiful place."

"Sorry to take you away from it for a while."

I nodded, but he didn't see me. He was watching the water. "It's all right, you know," I said.

"How's that?"

"I'm restless. You're right. Mentally I'm restless."

"It's Nicole, isn't it?" he asked.

"Is it? I'm afraid it's me, Lyel."

"I think you'd do well to find yourself a female distraction."

"Can you honestly say that you've ever used a woman in that way? As a distraction, I mean?"

"No. Never."

"Me neither. And I hope I never do."

"As more than a distraction, then."

I said nothing.

"What say we go work on that bottle of rum I brought back from the islands and explore the various aspects of this case."

"Have I ever told you you were psychic?"

"Many times," he said. "But rarely when we're sober."

He drove. I rode in silence. We rounded the corner by the Twisted Gorge mine. Still no sign of Broadmore. Only the barren gray field of mine tailings, and the stoic remains of the wooden aqueduct that had deposited them there.

4

Butte Peak's county courthouse is a three-story brick edifice built at the end of the Second World War. I drive a 1960 Ford half-ton pickup that had once been fire-engine red with white bumpers. "Old Red" was now an odd shade of orange, which had previously been the undercoating, with pockmarked bumpers a neglected rust brown. The truck boasted a mismatched set of leaf springs, so that it charged down the road at an angle that implied that the driver was overweight. The driver's door stuck badly; its hinge banged loudly upon opening and closing. It drew the attention of anyone and everyone within half a block. I'd been known to duck between parked cars to avoid being associated with the shrill pop it made.

On that day, there was no place to duck. I slammed it shut. It sounded like the report from a sixteen-inch gun. A woman in the courthouse hoisted a shade and peered out curiously, probably thinking someone had been shot. I waved. She pulled the shade back down quickly.

A ceiling fan stirred the air in the foyer on the main floor. I found records on the second floor, on the other side of a well-used L-shaped counter that kept *us* separated from *them*.

"Can I help you?" The heavy woman wore glasses

with the initial *R* etched into the lower corner of the right lens. Candy had mentioned a Rita; this had to be she. I wondered if she saw a reversed R superimposed on my face as she looked at me. Her neck was a cruel mixture of saturated fats and overindulgence, and her cheeks made her a cousin to Dizzy Gillespie. Her puffy lips were almost hidden by her cheeks, but she had painted them so bright a shade of red that I couldn't miss them. Some of the lipstick had skidded onto her two front teeth.

"I'm looking for Bert McGreggor—"

"Not here," she interrupted.

"No. I know that. I mean her sister has asked me to look for her, and I was wondering if I could speak to somebody about her."

She didn't approve. Or maybe she didn't understand. Maybe she couldn't hear. She squinted—apparently she couldn't see—and shook her head. "I don't see how," she said. "We can't just sit around and jaw, you know. This is a public office. We've got work to do. Hey, Mary!" she yelled at a woman hunched behind a desk. "What do I do if some guy wants to talk to us about Bert? He's looking for her."

"Everyone's looking for her," Mary replied. "Have him come back tomorrow."

"I don't think you understand," I tried, but Mary was having none of me. Someone had chained her paper clips together, and she was clearly flustered.

"Come back tomorrow," Rita said.

"Rita, don't be such a jerk," said a feisty little woman with lopsided eyes. She bumped Rita out of the way and grinned at me. "I'm Emma-Jean. What do you want to know?"

"Not on *my* time!" yelled Mary.

Emma-Jean was not intimidated. "No one ever gets fired from here," she allowed. "You have to retire, quit, or die. Now, what's this about Bert?"

Part of my mind was gauging how tight and firm a woman had to be to shape clothes the way this one did. "You saw her last Monday?" I asked.

"We all left at the same time on Monday, just after four-thirty. Same as always. Haven't seen her since."

"She hasn't called?"

"Nope. Haven't heard anything at all. She just up and vanished. We were guessing she might have run off with Nicky. They're hot and heavy, you know. But I hear Nicky hasn't seen her either."

"Did you know her very well?"

"Sure, I guess so." She shrugged. My eyes wandered down her. She noticed, but Emma-Jean wasn't bothered by it.

"Can you think of anything that might help me to locate her?"

"Listen, if Nicky can't find her—"

"Emma!" Mary complained.

"I'm talking to this gentleman," Emma-Jean objected loudly. "Don't worry about her," she advised me.

"Just what is it exactly that this office handles?" I asked her.

"Nothin'," she said coyly, giving me a wink. "Just kiddin'."

A man's voice came from behind me. Thickest western twang I had heard in ages. His words rolled together in a tongue-tangled slur, making it hard to understand him. "This office here handles the filing and recording of every kinda record you can think of. Water rights, births, deaths, voting records, voting registration, public auction notifications." He was a short man, messy gray hair, glasses that enlarged his eyes. He looked vaguely familiar to me.

"Land deeds, plat registration," Emma-Jean finished for him. "Mayor," she said in a tone of greeting.

Brandon Cousin nodded at her, his big eyes bulging even further, then nodded and smiled at me. "Need those minutes of last week's meeting, Emmy, if you don't mind."

"Heck of an accident yesterday, wasn't it, sir?" I asked him. Strange that I had been onstage as a musician in front of ten thousand people, confident and strong, yet here in the presence of a backwater mayor I felt uneasy and even a little bit in awe. "Chris Klick," I said, offering him my hand. "I'm a volunteer fireman. Sort of."

"Sort of, heck! Klick and Lyel. I heard from Steve Garman that you saved our veterinarian's life." He shook my hand vigorously. "Not to mention his live-in's." He winked. "Pleased to make your acquaintance. We're trying to think up some sort of award to give you boys. That was one heck of a thing, way I hear."

"An award? No, sir. We don't need an award. Steven and the boys deserve the awards."

"Not the way I hear it."

"We were lucky, weren't we?"

"Depends, son. Pilot wasn't so lucky. Those of us who want to keep the airport here in town don't consider ourselves lucky. No, I'd say our good luck has just about run out." He slapped me on the outside of my arm. He couldn't reach my shoulder comfortably, and he obviously felt like pounding me one in congratulations. It bothered me to like the man. I had read so many unsettling things about the airport, things I'd associated with Cousin, that I wanted to dislike him. He was full of the country-hick image, but his magnified eyes showed a good mind at work. Without looking at her, he reached out and accepted the papers from Emma-Jean. "Thanks, sweetheart," he said. His peripheral vision seemed symbolic to me: here was a man who knew what was going on around him.

"This man's trying to find Bert for us," Emmy said.

"For her sister," I corrected her.

Cousin squinted at me, despite the thick glasses. "Is that right?" he said after a heartbeat's pause. Then he

smiled graciously. "Well, somebody had better find that
girl pretty damn soon, or we're all likely to drown in
paperwork around here. Nice meeting you, Mr. Klick."
He slapped me on the arm again, a good ol' boy if ever
there was one.

"What exactly does Bert do here?" I asked.

"Work. Unlike *some* of us," Mary chided from her
desk.

"Same as the *rest* of us," Emma-Jean said, raising her
voice. "A little of this, a little of that. Whatever comes
in, mostly. Her specialty was land deeds."

"Her specialty in what way?"

"She understood land. She could glance at a property
description and tell you right where it was. You know—
the northeast quarter of the southwest section of parcel
forty-two. Land deeds are the *worst*!"

Just the mention of land set off an alarm inside me.
Land was money, power, mineral and water rights—
arguably the most desired possession.

"Did she like the job?" I asked.

"Did?"

"Does . . ." I corrected.

"I suppose she does. There're better jobs than this.
But there's no slack —you work full calendar, not like
with jobs in Snow Creek—the pay's fair, benefits decent. And like I said, once you got the job, ain't nobody
gonna take it away."

"That policy can always change, you know," Mary
remarked ominously.

"I better go," Emma-Jean said. I studied her backside
as she pumped her way past Mary's desk.

I avoided looking at Rita on my way out. I wanted that
image of Emma-Jean fresh in my mind.

5

Nick Young, grease smeared up to his elbows, wore his blond hair in a crew cut, and had two huge front teeth that were bleach white except for opposing yellow stains from the Marlboro glued to his lower lip. He squinted through the smoke when he talked. He was working on the valve cover of a Fairlane V-6, one of the most enduring cars ever built. This was a '65 or '66, and the engine, steam-cleaned and polished within an inch of its life, was beautiful. "Nice machine," I offered from a distance.

"Damn straight."

"Yours?"

"Damn straight."

"What's the problem?"

He looked up and squinted. "No problem. This here's my lunch hour. Just buffin' her out."

"She looks pretty buffed."

"Yeah," he agreed, glancing back at her like a proud father. "What can I do for you?"

I introduced myself. "Candy's asked me to try and find Bert."

His only response to that was a low grunt. I asked him about Bert.

"We've been going together about two years, I
guess," he told me in his dry, flat voice. "And now this."
"This?"
"Her walking out and all."
"Is that what this is about?" I asked.
"She ain't never pulled nothing like this. Not exactly.
But I'll tell you something, I don't put up with this kinda
shit." His tar-encrusted vocal cords made him sound
forty-five. He was probably closer to twenty-five.
"Then you think she's taken off somewhere? As op-
posed to having gotten herself in some sort of trouble."
"One in the same, if you ask me. Of course she's taken
off somewhere. And that's trouble. The question is, _who_
has she taken off with? If it's another girl, then it ain't so
bad I suppose. But if it's some guy . . ." His look finished the sentence for him.
"So I take it she's done it before, but not quite like
this," I stated, attempting to clarify.
"She likes to drive, ya know? She has a red Mustang.
Convertible. Brand new, all the extras. I put in the roll
bar myself. Every now and then she likes to just get in
and let it fly. Reno. Vegas. Jackpot. Or sometimes just to
race. She'll drive over to the INEL and drag against
those Arco boys."
The Idaho Nuclear Engineering Laboratory, near
Arco, Idaho, is home to fifty-four nuclear test reactors
and is a source of political controversy. It happens to
employ tens of thousands of people—mostly transplants
to the state. It has also been charged with dumping
millions of gallons of "low-level" nuclear waste into one
of the West's largest aquifers.
"Why the INEL?" I asked, not seeing where it fit in.
"The roads. You know, they bus all those guys in from
Idaho Falls every fucking day of the year."
"I still don't get it."
"The roads. Don't you know nothin'? With all that
heavy traffic, the highway busts up every year or two.

The feds provide the dough to lay fresh blacktop down. Goddamn. Must be what—fifty, sixty miles of perfect blacktop. Couldn't find a better drag strip."

What Nick didn't know was that one of my outside interests is modified Volkswagens. I turn them into dune buggies that can outdrag most stock cars. I've been racing off-road for the better part of fifteen years. Nick had probably been about ten when I started racing.

"You think she may have gone out to the INEL by herself? Would she do that?"

"I don't know. Maybe. It's all guys out there, and she's been a little hard on them. They don't like losing to a girl. I hope she didn't go out there. If those boys turned angry . . . I gotta think it was Vegas or something."

"But I can hear in your voice that you're not convinced."

"No, not really."

"Why's that?"

"Thing about it is, she's not the type to miss work. That ain't her style. She's real careful about that job. That woman likes money. That there is a damn good job, and she knows it."

"Have you and Bert had any trouble lately? Romance-wise?"

"Nah. None to speak of. It's not really smooth with Bert in the first place." He put a cigarette in his mouth, glancing over at me as he struck the match to see if I was looking at him, which I was. He looked back at the cigarette just as quickly. It stuck there on his lip. I wondered if it was magnetic. "I'll tell you one thing. Just when you think you got a girl figured out, she goes and fucks with your head. First your dick, then your head. Probably blew town to avoid repaying a loan. Either that or she was seeing some guy and setting me up. She's been kinda paranoid."

I had worked my way around to the front of the car so

I could watch him work. His fingers knew everything there was to know about that engine. It gave me the idea to write a musical where all the characters are parts of a car.

"Paranoid?" I asked.

"Nothing to it. She had been winning lately—at the tables, I mean. I mean *lots* of money. But she owes a few friends some money, okay? That got to her. She paid some people back, but not everybody. She thought people were going to come after her winnings and drain her. That's why I'm thinking Vegas. Why pay people back when you can gamble with it?"

Amazing logic. "How much money?" I asked. "What kind of friends?"

"Couple grand spread between eight, nine people. Are you trying to say that something bad happened to Bert? 'Cause I mean now you got me thinking about those guys out at the INEL getting pissed off at her, or some asshole around here demanding she make good on a loan and getting rough with her, and that's bad shit, man."

"Can you give me the names of the people she borrowed from?"

"I probably could if I thought about it, but she'd be pissed off at me if I did, and I just don't see it the way you do. So the answer is no. Listen, I admit this isn't exactly normal for her, but you gotta watch out for Candy. She's one of those overprotective sisters, you know? Those girls lost their mother when they were little, and Candy thinks she's the mama. You know the type?"

I glanced through the open back door of the large garage. It was a recently poured cement floor, a large expanse of clean gray. Poor man's marble. On the floor were a thousand black engine pieces. "What's going on in here?" I asked.

"You know that plane wreck?" Nick asked. He didn't

wait for me to acknowledge that I did; he obviously assumed everyone had heard about the plane wreck. He appeared glad to have the subject changed. "That there is the engine, or what's left of it. FAA guys needed a space to lay it all out. They got what's left of the plane over in one of the hangars, but they contract out the engine work, and we won the bid, on account we're the only game in town just about, and we got this new floor poured, and the guy from the FAA thought our floor was bitchin'."

"So what's going on?"

"The boss and I are cleaning her for him. Putting all the parts where they belong. The boss knows everything there is to know about airplane engines—knows everything there is to know about any kind of engine. He gets thirty bills an hour for this. I take twenty-five. That's fuckin' government work for you, right? Twice what we normally get."

"You clean it and then what?"

"They send some guy up from Salt Lake or Denver. Someplace. When it's all laid out, and cleaned up, then they send this guy in and he goes through it all, piece by piece, you know, to see what fucked up. But he won't find nothin'."

"Why do you say that?"

" 'Cause there's nothing there to find. Boss said so right away. Took a look at the parts, you know, maybe an hour into it he looks up and says to me that there ain't nothing wrong with this engine. Something else caused that crash. Probably mechanical, is what he thinks. He says he could have her running again with just a couple adjustments. And if that's what he says, then that's the way it is. You never seen a guy like my boss. He can listen to an engine for about ten seconds and tell you exactly what's wrong. Fuckin' guy is psychotic."

Psychic, I was about to say, but I let it go. Correcting a person's speech is not the best way to make friends.

* * *

Lyel met me for lunch at the Southside Deli. Gloria, the owner, fixed me a mock meatball sandwich, no cheese, with a pickle and a low-fat milk. Lyel had an eggplant Parmesan sandwich dripping with oil and extra cheese. I was convinced he did it just to goad me.

"You got that sandwich just to make me watch you eat it, didn't you?" I asked.

"You can't stay on a no-fat diet forever," he said.

"It's not a diet, it's a way of life. And it's low-fat, not no-fat. It's not something I'm going to suddenly give up. It's a life-style thing. I hate that word, but that's what it is."

"The no-fat life-style. Sounds like a book to me."

I ate.

"I spoke with Candice again this morning," Lyel said between greedy bites. He refused to call her Candy, claiming it made her sound like a Playboy bunny. "I asked about her sister's finances. Roberta evidently likes the gaming tables in Jackpot."

"Nick said as much."

"She also likes to shop. Candice wasn't sure, but she suspects she owes a good deal of money to a good number of people. I took the liberty of making a few phone calls. One was to a friend of mine at National Credit Bureau. Technically, it's illegal to give me that information, but who's getting technical?" Lyel had many such friends. I never asked him for the names, just as he never asked about my many contacts. "Roberta McGreggor owns nine credit cards, mostly out of state, all but two charged to their limit. Those two are local and were recently paid off. Oddly enough," he added, "getting the local information may be more difficult."

"So she's a credit card junkie."

"That's how it looks," he said.

I told him what Nick had passed along to me. "I'm thinking she disappeared to avoid her creditors."

"That doesn't make sense," he said. "Eventually you come back, and your creditors are still there."

"She's young. A lot of things seem to make sense at that age," I reminded him.

He wolfed his way into the sandwich. Oil dripped into his sandwich basket.

"If she doesn't want to be found, it won't be easy to find her," I suggested.

"You've found plenty of people who didn't want to be found."

"You expect me to follow through with this? Is that it, Lyel? Is that what you want? It seems to me we've all but ruled out foul play."

"We promised Candice."

"We promised we'd look into it. We want to look any further and we're going to need Roberta's credit card statements. We're going to need something to track her out of state."

"And I'll see what my local banker can do for us," he said. "I'm not without influence in this town, you know."

"An understatement. Influence? If you wanted to, my friend, you could probably *buy* one of these towns." He didn't appreciate the comment. "Listen, maybe she's gone off to someplace she's gone before," I tried. "People tend to use the same motels, eat at the same restaurants. If Candy could get us into Bert's place, maybe we could dig up her past statements, canceled checks, that kind of thing. It might give us a place to start." I hesitated. I knew he wouldn't like this. "Otherwise, I think we ought to give it a week or two and see if we have some better leads."

"I'll check with Candice. I'll make a few more calls." He slobbered his way through the rest of the sandwich. His napkin was orange with oil by the end of the meal.

6

After lunch I went fishing. The green drake hatch, the first major hatch of the season, had arrived and was rumored to be happening just below Butte Peak between the hours of eleven and three. Roger, a friend of Lyel's who's a fishing guide for one of the outfitters in Snow Lake, had caught three rainbows over twenty inches the day before. That kind of tale was enough to get me moving.

I returned home to fetch my gear. It was a ramshackle collection of equipment, some of it given to me, some of it on permanent loan, some of it purchased. As my fishing technique had improved, albeit slowly, I'd begun to long for quality gear. There's a substantial difference between the response of a fiberglass rod and that of a graphite, or the handling of a twenty-dollar reel and a two- or three-hundred-dollar one, or the comfort of one set of waders and another. Two years prior I would have scoffed at such talk, but now I know better, and as I put my crummy piecemeal gear into the back of my pickup, I debated spending some of my nine grand. I quickly decided against it: money is to be saved, not spent. Lyel feels different. He spends money like the rest of us use oxygen.

I parked the truck by a new set of public tennis courts

on the south side of Butte Peak. There is a bend in the river there, just below the steep rocky rise of Glenda's Ridge, a sheer rockface that climbs out of the river and reaches toward the clouds. I battled with my waders, put on my vest and my polarized sunglasses, and headed into the water.

I collected my thoughts, rethinking the several steps of a good cast. Lifting the rod, I fed my line out and finally presented the fly.

That was when a fish hit: right on the first cast. It slammed the fly at the end of the nearly invisible tippet. The reel screamed loudly as the line fed out, allowing the fish to run. It was a rainbow, a male, judging by the full color, and it came out of the water like a bucking bronco comes out of the chute, twisting and writhing and doing everything in its power to shake that hook out.

I had set the hook well, and he stayed with me. He splashed back into the rushing water and came out again just as quickly. I lifted the tip of the rod even higher, keeping my angle correct. His weight combined with the power of the river to work against me; it felt as if I had hooked a bucket. The rod bent into a question mark and off he went again, first running with the river, demanding additional line, then abruptly reversing himself and returning. My hand cramping, I cranked the reel furiously, attempting to keep slack out of the line, and sidestepped to my left to maintain some semblance of an angle between the two of us.

My attention fixed on the end of the tippet, I fought the fish, sensing the strength of the minuscule line, giving to the fish when necessary, taking line when the fish was generous enough to offer it to me.

We played back and forth, give and take, for about ten minutes—it felt more like half an hour. Then I had him. He was exhausted, and he began rising to the surface and just lying there, letting the white water boil over

him. He was a beauty, with a large fluorescent pink
brushstroke down his middle and a silver sheen to his
skin. I reeled him in. He had nothing left. I netted him,
wetted my hands, and held him gently while I removed
the barbless hook from his hard jaw. He was about fifteen inches, maybe two pounds: a good solid fish. A nice
fish. A fish to be proud of. I held him under, facing him
upstream in the water until I saw his gills working well,
and then I turned him loose. One shake of his tail and he
was gone, a silver blur disappearing into the translucent
water.

I stood there for a moment, the pleasant sound of the
river in my ears, heart pounding from the adrenaline.
The first fish of the season is an incredible experience. I
cherished it.

Then my thoughts returned to Bert McGreggor. She
was out there somewhere, just as this fish had been out
there. The trick with fish was to know what stretch of
river they liked and to present something to them that
they needed and wanted: food. In Bert's case, it would
be money.

After returning home, I solicited Lyel's company, and
he joined me on the deck to further explore what steps
needed to be taken to track Bert's travels by means of
her credit trail, expanding on our discussion over lunch.
He had made a few calls locally, hoping to gain access to
her checking accounts, but to little effect.

"Mimi wasn't in," he explained of the bank manager
with whom he had a close professional relationship. Lyel's vast holdings—East Coast family money supple-
mented by a hefty salary during his years as an NBA
strong forward—required a base of operations for investment purposes. In the East, it was New York City;
the West, San Francisco; but in Butte Peak, Idaho, it was
the Western Rockies Savings Bank, where the manager,
Mimi Huck, treated Lyel like a Rockefeller. "She's off

for the next few days, which leaves Wendy, and you have a better thing going with Wendy than I do."

"Wendy is a saint. But I have no deposits, friend. And she is certainly too ethical to dig up a record of canceled checks based on looks and charm. It would take Norton's help, and we don't have nearly enough evidence to involve the sheriff's office. In fact, given everything so far—which is basically nothing—I'm far more interested in this plane accident than the 'disappearance' of Bert McGreggor."

"Now don't go straying on me, Klick."

"I'm not straying, I'm *stating*. She is the one straying. Facts, Lyel. Candy's fears are not supported by fact. Bert's boyfriend admits she has wandered off before."

"Not for this long," he pointed out.

But I was going now, and there was no stopping me. "Records are set every day, Lyel. Especially in the game of love."

"The trouble with you, Klick," he said, sipping some beer, "is that you tend to sound like you're quoting the Four Tops."

"Live by the lyric, die by the lyric."

"Yes. Exactly right. I fear you often do the latter."

"Don't change the subject. If Bert is true to her past, then she's living off credit cards."

"What if we find she isn't?" he asked.

"We'll cross that bridge if and when we get there. But even if we find the cards aren't being used, that's not proof of much. Her boyfriend said she had been in the chips lately—literally—so she could be living off her cash."

"A trip to a few of her favorite gambling halls might be in order. Casinos are plenty familiar with repeat customers; they would know if she had been around."

"They *might* know," I replied. "Okay, while you're working on Wendy," I told him, "I'll call a few casinos and check up on her."

From where we sat, I saw a rippled V interrupt the slough's mirror surface. I recognized that V. There are few fish that can leave such an enormous wake. "Zeus," I announced.

Lyel looked out and nodded solemnly in agreement; he too knew that wake. "Well?" he asked. Then he stated, "It's sporting time," in an affected voice and with an enthusiasm that brought him out of his chair. I retrieved my rod from the bed of Old Red and hurried to the slough. Lyel snagged two more beers and joined me. The wake had abruptly stopped about ten feet beyond the dense willow to my right, indicating a dive. Tracking Zeus was like tracking a submarine. I floated the line overhead, feeding it out slowly, the loop of leader and tippet uncurling softly at the end of each go.

At last I presented the fly atop the mirrored surface, a feather falling from the sky. I find slow water much more difficult to fish, for if the fly is not presented correctly, the line handled delicately, the smart fish see the ruse for what it is. And Zeus is one smart fish. The fly must float down from the sky exactly as would a dying insect and must appear to Zeus or his brethren as though God intended it to be eaten. I tried five more casts.

"Bingo!" Lyel shouted loudly in my ear as Zeus rose out of the water on the end of my line. I felt as if I had accidentally hooked an otter. My reel emitted an incredibly high-pitched whine as the line fed out. I knew the sound of my equipment, like a driver knows the sound of a vehicle's engine. That huge wake again sliced a crack into the surface of the slough, and I briefly experienced what Ahab must have felt. Zeus resurfaced, proud, defiant, and snapped his hard body vigorously, attempting to shake the hook.

The whine suddenly stopped. I glanced down to see that line had backed into the faulty reel. Badly tangled, it knotted and the line would no longer feed. The tippet broke, and Zeus, free once again, dove for the bottom. My rod straightened. I looked over at Lyel, feeling the frustration and anger boiling into my face. He looked down disapprovingly at my reel. Derby barked from some unseen hole she had dug in the pasture.

"Cheap shit," Lyel said, still eyeing the reel. He had been telling me this for weeks.

I threw rod, reel, line, and leader into the slough. It splashed, faltered momentarily, and disappeared from sight.

And there it remains.

7

Lyel and I spent the next day mutually pursuing Bert McGreggor. Candy claimed to have tried but failed to locate her sister's credit card bills, or canceled checks, and although Lyel had offered my services in this regard, Candy suggested she give it one more try, which to both Lyel and me meant she had forgotten to do so in the first place. People have funny ways of covering their oversights.

For my part, I spent the first half of my day at the Snow Lake Community Library with the ever cooperative Ellie, who helped me locate and photocopy the appropriate sections of yellow pages for the Nevada cities of Reno, Jackpot, and Las Vegas. After a low-fat lunch at Perry's Sandwich Shop—not an easy feat, given the mayonnaise-laden temptations—I returned to the cabin and began phoning various gaming establishments. To my disappointment, none had ever heard of a Roberta McGreggor, and I realized our error in judgment: she was far too much a penny-ante player to have gained the attention or recognition of the houses. She could have been right at the blackjack table as we spoke, and they would have been none the wiser. Still, I made all my calls, every single one, if for no other reason than that I needed ammunition to use against Lyel.

In my opinion, the woman, cash warming her pocket, up to her knees in IOUs, had fled town without notice in hopes of gambling her way to newfound wealth. Translated: she would be home when the money ran out, and a likely candidate for Gamblers Anonymous. For all of her sister's concern—and I was factoring in Nick's description of Candy as overbearing and maternal—I had not unearthed a single piece of evidence to indicate foul play.

Perhaps that is why when a stranger named Alicia Gebhardt called at eight-fifteen the next morning and invited me to a business breakfast, I accepted. I asked what kind of business, and she said my kind of business. Music? I asked. Missing persons? Sort of, I was told. Ten o'clock she said. I was looking for an out on this McGregor thing; perhaps this would be it.

I knew the address. Very chichi. A California transplant, no doubt. But chichi means bucks, and though I don't like to hire out to that kind of people and in fact didn't really want the work, it seemed a possible transition from a nagging Lyel back to the sprinkler system, the slough, and runs with Derby. Lyel would respect the prospect of a paying job—at least, I allowed myself to believe he would, though I certainly didn't phone him and tell him I was heading off in search of such work.

"Have you any idea how long this work might take?" I asked the kind, youthful voice.

"A couple of days maybe. I don't really know."

"In town?"

"Out of town," she replied. "I'd rather explain in person."

She couldn't see me smile, but I was damn near dancing with glee. It seemed too good to be true.

It turned out, much later, that it was.

* * *

A few minutes out of Ridland I slowed and pulled Old
Red off the highway into a widened spot in the road
used as a temporary weigh station. The hay fields of the
Flying Heart Ranch were what had caught my attention. From the whitewashed fence by the old farmhouse, north to the southern edge of the runway
stretched what seemed to be wilted hay. Thirty, maybe
forty acres' worth. I recalled seeing frantic Mexican
workers out in the field on the day of the fire. They had
been spraying the crop, using long lengths of garden
hose, attempting (I thought then) to extinguish *fire*. But
what I saw here had not been caused by fire—it appeared more chemical in nature—and so forced me to
reevaluate what I had witnessed that morning. Not a
fan of coincidence, I couldn't help but connect the wilt-
ing crop to the plane crash. No time. I jumped back into
the truck and drove on.

* * *

110 Fairways Road. The mailbox, adorned with hand-
painted ducks landing in bulrushes, read: A. GEBHARDT.
Alicia? I wondered. Was all this hers? The sprawling
home—several thousand square feet of it—overlooked
Snow Lake's eighteen-hole golf course. The ostentatious
roof was of pounded copper, the outside woodwork of
burly maple in a nailless construction using butterfly
joints and dowels. The door, koa wood, displayed a
hand-carved scene of a woman standing atop a mountain overlooking Snow Lake. The replication was perfect. A single piece of copper embedded in the carving
represented the roof of the house I was about to enter.
As I studied the scene more closely, the door opened.
The *A* stood for Anthony, "Tony Gebhardt," as he intro-

duced himself. Bronzed, small, and almost handsome. He reached out, snatched my hand, and squeezed it vigorously, letting me know that at fifty-something he still felt seventeen. I felt a little uneasy. He reminded me of Robert Conrad. I have never been a fan.

The foyer floor was like a runway of pink marble. A five-foot-high ebony elephant guarded the first step of the unsupported stairway. A Nike windbreaker hung from one of the plastic tusks. Real ivory was not chichi. Tony Gebhardt wore the pants that matched. Directly ahead, a six-foot teak totem pole marked the entrance to the sunken living room. I expected an appearance by Marlin Perkins at any moment.

"Fiji," he said as he caught me admiring it. I hadn't asked.

The living room contained similar hand-carved pieces from Asia and the South Pacific. Much of the furniture was hidden by a jungle of house plants. I sponged my way across the carpet, which felt like woven quicksand, finally making it safely out onto the flagstone patio. The house was built in a U, with two long arms defining an enormous courtyard, of which the patio was but one small part. Gebhardt led me to a redwood table. At the far end of the house's right wing stood a large glass-walled pavilion.

By the look of him, Gebhardt had some Spanish or Italian blood in him. Dark-featured, the bronze skin came to him naturally. His upper teeth were pushed in slightly, making him look as if he had attempted to bite a steel pipe as a kid. He had an abundance of hair, very manly, and dark, somewhat savage brown eyes. He seated me to his right, with a good view of the fairway, where a gentleman in bright green pants and a salmon shirt made a poor attempt at a pitch onto the green. It fell short. So did Gebhardt in my esteem: short man's complex. Something wrong about him.

"Do you play?" he asked me.

I replied, "What I do with golf clubs should certainly
not be called playing. I hack, I chop, I butcher, leaving
divots deep enough to hide golf carts. I generally use up
my par on the green alone. Off the tee I'm dynamite. I
love the game, but it is not a relationship based on
mutual respect."

"We should play sometime. I live here, on the course,
but I can't play at all."

"He's a liar; he's a scratch golfer." The voice from the
phone call. Wife or daughter? She came onto the patio
from behind me, and so I didn't see her at first; I smelled
her, a delightful combination of spring flowers. Daughter. Had to be. Same dark, intriguing eyes. Young, vi-
brant, confident. She wore a cotton turquoise sundress.
Flawless skin the color of oiled walnut. She was round-
faced with a small nose and oddly twisted ears. She
should have used her thick hair to hide those ears.

The staging was marvelous: this was living—at least
that's what television would lead you to believe, I
thought. I wouldn't have traded Lyel's cabin for any of
this. There was an arrogance about this kind of showy
wealth. It had been taken to its limit and then some. I
longed to be back with Derby and a bowl of cereal.

"So?" I asked. There are no free lunches—or break-
fasts—I reminded myself. "Why exactly am I here?"

A sectioned grapefruit sat on each of the plates, a
stemless, pitted fresh cherry in the center. Alicia turned
to her father to answer me.

"We read about you in the local paper not long ago,"
Gebhardt said.

"You and Lyel," she said, making him sound like a
close friend of hers. I didn't ask how she knew him; Lyel
knew all the Fairways set.

"We need to trace the ownership of a building," Gebhardt explained. "It's kind of a race, I'm afraid, and we'd
like to win it."

Alicia took over. "About a year ago, my father and I

bought controlling interest in a company that had been manufacturing sails for very small pleasure craft. We both love to wind-surf, and a good friend of mine, a creative genius actually, had developed a fantastic new board design for wave jumping. It's really big in Maui. Father and I built a company around him. We bought the sail company and retro-fitted the equipment to produce sails for wind-surfing. Then we arranged for an awful lot of equipment so we could begin producing the boards. That was when Jimmy, our designer, fell in love. Moved south of San Francisco and married the girl."

Gebhardt said, "Refuses to work with us unless we locate the manufacturing plant within twenty miles of his new home. No shit," he added. "He's giving us ultimatums after we've sunk over forty K into this thing!"

"We have no hold over him. The design is complete, but we want Jimmy to oversee production," Alicia continued.

I felt as if I was watching a tennis tournament, my eyes going left, right, left, right. These two were quite a pair.

A young Hispanic woman delivered strawberry waffles and a plate of scrambled eggs with Brie and scallions. Gebhardt served himself and passed the platters on to me as Alicia added, "There is a warehouse in an industrial complex, and it has everything we're looking for. My father sets his sights on something and look out!"

Gebhardt said, "Not just any warehouse will do. We need proximity to shipping; we require a certain size, with room for expansion and available light. There are a few dozen criteria, not to mention Jimmy's requirements.

"I don't know how much you know about industrial space on the coast, Chris, but it's increasingly difficult to find. The stuff that's any good is. You look confused," he remarked.

Alicia continued for him. I was getting seasick. "Let

me explain. We hired someone local from down there to try and trace the owners of this warehouse. I mean it's the *only* warehouse that's going to work for us."

"It's tangled up in some legal crap," Gebhardt said, interrupting.

"We're of the opinion he's stringing us out just to earn his daily fee."

"That's why you pay bonuses upon completion," I said. My comment caused a momentary silence. It didn't last long.

Through a mouthful of food Gebhardt said, "Speaking of money, you operate for what—fifteen, twenty percent?"

"Actually, twenty-five, but—"

"Twenty-five percent, fine. We'd pay you a healthy per diem plus twenty-five percent of what amounts to a forty-day assembly backlog, which this downtime has cost us. Your share would work out to . . . what? About twelve and a half."

"Hundred?"

"Heavens no," Alicia said. "Thousand."

It's not often that I am at a complete loss for words. I can usually manage a grunt or a groan. I sipped some fresh-squeezed orange juice. I had received other offers for PI work—usually divorce stuff—but the pay had been minor league. How hard could it be to trace the owners of a Bay Area warehouse?

"Are you finished?" she asked, noticing my cooling food. I hadn't touched it.

"It's a fantastic offer, it really is. It's just that I don't do this kind of thing."

Gebhardt countered; it felt as if he had prepared for my response. "You find people, don't you? Musicians . . . and for a percentage. We want you to find who owns this warehouse."

"It's different," I said. I was losing ground and we all knew it.

"How?" he asked.

Suddenly, under the penetrating gaze of those dark eyes of his, I wasn't so sure. I grinned. They were both staring at me, and the twelve thousand was beginning to take effect.

Gebhardt sensed my softening. "Tell you what. Take a minute to think about it."

"How about a swim?" Alicia asked. She hadn't touched her food either. Some breakfast.

"You could borrow one of my suits," Gebhardt offered.

Alicia said, "Yes, why don't we cool off?"

It was much too fast for me. The twelve thousand was still stealing my wits. She left the table. I rose like an automaton, eyes glued to a smiling Anthony Gebhardt.

"Chris?" he called after me when I headed toward the living room, instead of toward the pool.

I turned back. "It's a generous offer. No question about that."

"What then?" Gebhardt asked.

"You two . . . you're like George and Gracie. You've got it all covered don't you?"

"Did we leave something out?"

"I doubt it. That's just the point."

"Listen," he said, thinking for me. "You came all the way up here from Ridland. You must be somewhat interested." It bothered me the way people in Snow Lake seemed to think of Ridland as being in another state. It's a twenty-five-minute drive. "The money's right; you just admitted as much."

"Why don't you tell the guy you hired to shit or get off the pot? Why don't you hire someone else from down there? There are some unanswered questions here, Mr. Gebhardt." My tone, harsh and unpleasant, turned his face red. *Why me?* I wanted to add. Why did he look scared to see me leaving?

For a brief moment he seemed stumped. Then he said, "You didn't eat a thing."

"None of us did," I pointed out.

"Well, Ali, she eats like a bird. Nothing to that. Sit back down. Let's eat. Come on!" he said, jiggling a chair. His near desperate tone bothered me. He sounded like a hawker at a county fair who needed gas money to reach the next town—step right up! I returned to the table and stood leaning against the back of the chair.

"The guy we hired got hurt," Gebhardt said somberly. "We don't know if it had to do with his work or not," he added hastily. "That's why the high fee, that, and because we're in a hurry. You want to take your friend Lyel along, that's okay. Fee remains the same, but I'll cover his expenses."

"I'm not sure I see why," I said.

"The thing of it is, you don't know my daughter. Ali is going to go do this herself. This downtime . . . This is her first real go at something. She's as impatient as her old man. You see? What price would you put on your daughter's safety? What if the trouble this guy had *was* related to his inquiries?"

"I'm not a baby-sitter."

"She's not exactly a baby. I just don't want her doing this alone. I need someone like you."

"But she's part of the deal?"

"She's going to go. I can't stop her from going. I'd like to. Why don't you speak to her? See what you think."

I had already seen, and what I saw interested me. Strangely enough, that was part of my resistance. That, and the way Lyel would take all of this.

"Pool's a great temperature," Gebhardt said.

* * *

She moved very well in the water, effortlessly graceful. Sunlight streamed in through the glass. At the far end

she tucked, executed an efficient somersault, and
sprang off the wall, thrusting back toward me underwa-
ter. She surfaced in a competent backstroke, her long
arms and pointed fingers reaching and pulling at the
clear blue water. She approached the shallow end
where I stood on the deck watching. My shadow crossed
her and she pulled up short, tipping her head back,
arching her chest toward me, and dipping her hair in
the water to draw it off her face. As she stood up, she
asked, "Well, did he talk you into it?" Then, "Aren't you
going to join me? The suit's in there."

She was a controller. I told myself to leave. But for
some reason I didn't listen to me, I listened to her. First
mistake. I turned around and pushed through the door
marked GUYS. The locker room had two short benches,
pegs on the wall, and a toilet stall at the far end. I
opened the frosted door on my left: a common shower
area of blue and yellow tile, with recessed lighting and
four shower heads. The frosted door opposite me led to
GALS.

I found a suit hanging from one of the shower heads.
Twelve and a half thousand dollars, I reminded myself.
Well managed, enough for a six-month retirement. To
people like Gebhardt, pocket change. The suit barely
fit. I bulged.

"Perfect," she said as I came out.

I dived in and did several laps. The water felt great. I
realized I was swimming hard and strong for her sake,
and I wondered at my ambitions. Annoyingly, I felt too
predictable. When I stopped at the shallow end, she was
sitting on the cement lip of the pool, leaning back on
her outstretched arms, aiming herself at me.

It had been eight months since Nicole had come and
gone in my life, but her image stayed with me, lingering
like the pulsing yellow orb that echoes a camera's flash. I
remained partially blind and was unsure exactly why.
Seeing Alicia—wanting her—reminded me of my loss.

She smiled warmly, sparkling in the sunlight as if covered with jewels. "What do you think of the offer?" she asked.

"Attractive," I said.

Her smile held me. Was she trying to tell me something, or were my hormones on seek and destroy? She seemed to read my mind. "Your fee is worth it to us. We wouldn't make the offer if it wasn't."

"And where do you fit in?"

She slapped her legs together unconsciously, and I was distracted. I was standing closer to her now, waist deep in the pool. I didn't remember having moved toward her. I had the odd sensation that I had not walked but had been drawn to her. The tiny, nearly invisible hairs on her breastbone were bleached white. Her breathing was smooth and regular. Droplets of water fell from her hair onto her shoulders, disappearing into the suit.

"We would be working together," she put forth, "if that's what you're asking. That is, as long as I wouldn't be interfering."

"You wouldn't interfere," I insisted, and felt suddenly foolish. Perhaps she would. Perhaps she was already.

"Will you take the job?"

"It's tempting," I admitted. Twelve thousand—even Lyel would understand that.

"Good."

"I am working on something else at the moment. I'll have to see."

"We have to get going on this right away; I'm afraid that's part of the deal."

I nodded. Gebhardt had made the time factor clear enough.

She reached out toward me. It was one of those gestures that would have been rude to avoid. I placed my hands below her rib cage and took hold of her firmly. She placed her fingers lightly on my shoulders and grinned again. I lifted her up and pulled her toward me, lowering her into the water. She seemed weightless. I hadn't felt a woman between my hands in quite some time.

"How about a race?" she asked. When I hesitated she added, "A push off the wall for a start. You'd cream me on the dive."

"You'll get me on the turn," I complained.

"I've got to have *some* advantage," she said.

You have all the advantage, I thought. "No stakes?" I teased.

"Sure," she said. "If I win, you take the job. If you win . . . well, you won't win. Ready?" she asked, backing up against the pool's wall.

I wasn't ready, and she knew it. "Go," she said, dropping down quickly and pushing off strongly, buttocks squeezing together tightly, sinewy legs stretching long.

I scrambled to a start, no time to move to the wall and get a push. I simply lunged forward and swam hard to catch up. Her feet were churning the water off to my left. She was fast. I kicked harder and pulled, pulled, pulled. Gasping for air, I saw that my head was even with her waist now. Forced to glance ahead to see how close I was to the turn, I lost a stroke. Had I been more practiced, I would have used the paint on the bottom of the pool. Her hind side disappeared. I fumbled through the turn and had to work like hell even to reach her ankles by the finish line.

"I cheated," she apologized.

"You won," I told her honestly.

She pushed away from the wall, sidestroking idly. "So?"

"I can't give you an answer today. I'll have to think about it."

"How about a shower and a cup of espresso?" she asked, swimming over to the edge and climbing easily out of the pool. Her efforts pulled her suit up to where it showed a tan line, and there wasn't much of a suit there to begin with. "Can't leave the chlorinated water on you," she explained. "It chaps your skin." She didn't wait for a reply but walked gracefully over to the door marked GALS, glanced over her shoulder and disappeared inside.

I opened the door to GUYS. I heard the opposing shower door thump closed, followed by the distinctive sound of a wet bathing suit hitting tile. She was in there, naked, a few feet away through the frosted glass. I heard the water run. Then a knock on my frosted door. "Decent?" she asked, popping open the door and sticking her head through.

She was standing close enough to the glass that her naked body appeared as a shapely, slightly blurred female form. Only slightly blurred. "Me first," she said. "Be out in a minute. Feels wonderful," she said as steam rose over the door and billowed down toward the floor.

I'll bet it does, I thought.

My imagination was spreading soap all over those firm curves. I heard the water stop and the opposing door bump shut. "Your turn," she hollered.

She was right about the shower: it felt great.

Her suit, balled up in a tiny clump, lay at my feet. I picked it up and held it by a strap at arm's length, studying it as water drained from its seams. I hung it on a hook.

"I think it would be fun," she told me loudly from the other side of the door. "To work together, I mean."

Her bronzed form again fluttered on the far side of her shower door. The white of her busy towel broke up the shifting flesh-colored shapes, and for some reason reminded me of the matador's cape. *Charge*, it commanded. I obeyed: I knew I would accept the offer.

Fun? I wondered. Fun I could handle.

Her I wasn't so sure about.

8

I didn't catch the man's name, but I thought he said Raúl. He was Mexican, about five foot seven, and somewhere between twenty-five and forty. His face had been creased by the sun, giving him the skin of a dried apricot. Most of his teeth were chipped or missing. He tilted his head when speaking to me, a disconcerting gesture that caused me to feel off balance. His jeans were filthy, his T-shirt stained at the armpits, and he had a sweat-matted red bandanna tied around his neck.

I liked him immediately. He spoke with the dry, rough voice of a two-pack-a-day man and offered me a genuine smile of congeniality. "Fucking shit kilt the crop."

"I saw you out there with hoses."

"Yeah. Sure. Mr. Tanner said to get it off the hay as fast as we could, so that's what we done. Right? But it no make no difference. Kilt it just the same."

"The plane that crashed," I stated.

He shrugged. "None of us seen which one done it. Christopher, my boy Christopher, named after Saint Christopher, God bless him, smelt it. He tell me about it. Listen man, Mr. Tanner a good man. He not only pay us, he give us extra if we bring in a good crop. Now, no extra."

He reached into his back pocket, retrieved a crumpled pack of Camels, found a broken cigarette, tore it cleanly in two, and stuck the longer half between his lips. Absentmindedly he flicked the tip of a wooden match with his thumbnail and lit up. From where I stood it looked like the flame singed his nose hairs.

"Smelled what?" I asked. "Pesticides?"

"Pesticides? Shit, no! Gasoline, man. Maybe a leak or somet'ing like that. Who knows, man?"

"Awfully big leak," I pointed out skeptically. It looked more like fuel dumping to me. And if it was fuel dumping, then it would be more visible, more apparent, from the air.

He missed my cynicism. "Fucking right," he said, exhaling a thick gray cloud and catching some of it with his nose.

* * *

Steven Garman, the fireman-sometimes-charter-pilot, agreed to trade me an hour in the air for an evening of trout fishing on the slough.

I had become a birder on one of my Idaho visits, not by design but by circumstance. The pastime grew on me. Hooked, I bought binoculars, then a high-powered monocular. I became starved for first light, when the first melodies crack the silence of dawn and the great blue herons pass overhead like gliders, their six-foot wingspans casting enormous shadows on the lawn.

In the process, I came to admire flight. I had come to experience every plane ride as an extraordinary, almost supernatural experience.

We met outside Snow Lake Aviation. I climbed into Steven's single-engine Cessna. We took off and headed south.

The damage to Flying Heart's hay crop was immediately apparent. Although the hay was not yet brown, delayed perhaps by the efforts of Raúl and his crew, by all appearances it soon would be. I pointed out the damaged crop to Steven.

"I doubt that's from dumping," he said loudly over the roar of the engine. "What happens is the commercial and corporate jets really tromp on it going out of here. They like to gain a lot of altitude quickly to clear those hills over by Twisted Gorge. What you see there could be heat damage, or even wind damage from the jets. Or it could be fuel," he admitted, briefly raising my hopes, "but in the form of exhaust. Bad mixture. Too rich. And if that's the case, it could have been anybody —could be *everybody*, cumulative effect, flight after flight spreading their exhaust day after day."

"Ranch hand said he could smell the fuel," I said.

"Maybe," Steven said, but he didn't sound convinced. "Why do you care anyway? Something you're working on?"

"I'm bothered by the pilot jumping for it. Doesn't add up."

"I know what you mean about that. Have to be some kind of stuntman to jump from a plane when you're taxiing."

A stuntman? It was something I hadn't considered, and yet somehow it made a lot more sense of things. To Steven it had been an offhand remark, to me, a possibility worth considering.

"But your theory doesn't make much difference anyway, Chris. Plane he was flying isn't set up to jettison fuel. He couldn't have been dumping if he'd wanted to."

"Unless he customized his rig for just that purpose," I pointed out. I couldn't be sure if Steven gave that any thought. He banked the plane gently over Ridland and showed me a great view of Lyel's property. I glanced back over his shoulder, hoping beyond reason to see more evidence of the jettisoned fuel, perhaps in the fields across from Flying Heart, but I saw none. Discouraged, I asked if we might fly beyond Ridland to the south and continue the search.

"The problem is this," Steven explained, agreeably directing the plane toward Poverty Flats, taking Rattlesnake Butte off our right wing. "Even if your theory is right, and I admit that although unlikely, it's *possible*, it is an insidious, even ingenious plot because the nature of fuel is that it dissipates quickly into the atmosphere. Given any altitude at all it won't reach the ground as a fluid. Let's say, for instance, that the late pilot *intended* to crash his plane—which is your suggestion—or knew in advance he had problems, a more acceptable explanation to a pilot—"

"Although the latter wouldn't explain his rigging the plane to dump fuel," I finished, knowing where he was headed. In the roar of the engine we were having to raise our voices to the point that my throat was beginning to feel sore. Steven seemed more used to it. Birds, I thought, did not have this problem.

"That the plane was rigged has yet to be proved," he reminded me. "Anyway, let's say he knew in advance. Let's say he *could* dump fuel. Then out here somewhere," he said, spreading his hand like a priest over a congregation, "he would have emptied all but a fraction of his tanks. At altitude, the liquid fuel reverts to a gas, doing no visible damage to the crops and foliage below. He approaches the airport," Steven said, reversing the plane abruptly, deciding we had seen enough. We retraced the dead pilot's route as Steven narrated. He radioed the airport and warned them he would do a touch-and-go before circling once and landing. The airport operator acknowledged. "We're about two miles out. Now, if it's to be an intentional crash, he's got a lot to do. First," Steven said, demonstrating, "he unstrapped. He's going to be busy with the controls on landing, and he won't have time then." I could picture the pilot; it wasn't Steven flying, but the man whom I had last seen with a pipe through his chest. It was as if I were watching a movie, and suddenly I felt as if I weren't in the plane at all.

Steven continued, "He would probably unlatch his door as well, though air speed would hold it firmly closed." Steven did this also. "Then he begins his approach, reviewing both the aborted landing he plans and checking his fuel gauge one last time. He wants the thing bone dry, don't forget. Only a born fool would intentionally trash a landing with fuel on board, I don't care *how* much they pay you. There's the airport up ahead."

My heart was pounding wildly in anticipation despite Steven's calm voice. "What I've heard is that he came in on one wheel, damn near dragging the right wing. The left wheel bounced a couple of times but he couldn't keep it down. That's a scary stunt; if he blows it, he's going to cartwheel, come part, and lose his chance to jump. But if he pulls it off, investigators might rule a stuck flap."

The plane slowed; its nose rose and floated toward the runway. Steven's hands and feet worked in what to me was choreographed confusion. His door thumped like a screen door before a violent storm.

"He dumps the rest of his fuel *now*!" he barked, reaching down to do so, "and leaves the valve open." He was a flurry of activity, and I nearly averted my eyes from the runway looming frighteningly close. The engine coughed. He said, "I've leaned the fuel ratio to effect nearly the same thing."

"Steven," I said shakily, thinking this was a little too exact an imitation. He didn't respond. The plane nicked the runway, our right wing nearly touching. We lifted and fell again, and again. Steven was a study in concentration. I felt ill and knew for sure my face must be bloodless.

Two people ran outside from the Snow Lake Aviation office, even though we had radioed. We blurred past them. Steven pushed against his door. It opened. He kept us angled up on just the one wheel, the wing dangerously low. He shouted, "Slow down enough that the door will open." Again he demonstrated. The engine died. Steven leveled us out; both wheels were on the runway but we were racing too fast to stop before the impending chain-link fence, which still bore the gash from the dead man's plane. Steven fiddled with knobs. The engine caught, raced; we gained speed. We lifted, easily clearing the fence and the burnt remains of the former gas station beyond it. Steven smiled and glanced over at me.

We circled and landed. As we were climbing out of the plane he spoke for the first time. "It could have been done, Chris. I think we just proved that. I wouldn't have believed it, I don't think, but I do now."

A car raced up and squealed to a stop. I recognized the angry red face of the man behind the wheel as that of Mayor cum Airport Manager Brandon Cousin. He jumped out of his car and shouted at Steven in his Western drawl, "Just what the hell you think you're doing?"

"A touch-and-go," Steven stated calmly.

"That was no touch-and-go," the mayor objected. "You son of a bitch, doing stunts at my airport. We just lost a pilot, didn't we? You think this is some sort of playground? I'll ground you, Garman, goddamn it! You're not going to fly that way in my airport."

"It was my fault," I interjected. "I was curious about the crash the other day. There was some fuel spilled onto the crops at Flying Heart. There's a possibility the crash was intentional."

"Intentional?" he said to me. "This is a matter for the FAA, not some Hollywood gumshoe. I won't have any of it at my airport."

"Yes, sir," Garman said as Cousin reached the car. He

flashed Garman an angry look, climbed in, and drove away fast.

"Sir?" I said. Garman wasn't the type to kowtow.

He looked worried. "You don't know him, Chris. He takes this airport very seriously. He swings one hell of a big stick. And I, for one, don't want to be hit by it. We'd all do better not to rile Cousin."

As we walked back toward the terminal, I asked, "Where are they keeping the wreckage?"

"Took the engine into town someplace. What's left of the fuselage is in that middle hangar." He pointed across the tarmac.

"Anybody guarding it?"

"Chris . . ."

"Is there?"

"It's locked up."

"But is anybody guarding it?"

He shook his head. "I doubt it. Cousin hired a couple of guys to police the airport in general."

"And if a person wanted to get inside, when would be the best time?"

"You can't poke around in a federal investigation. Didn't you hear the man? Stay out of it."

"Thanks," I said.

* * *

The Idaho air is perfumed by thousands of acres of sage, by the great greenbelts of cottonwoods that form shaded lanes along the rivers' edges, by the copses of aspen and dense hedges of lilac and honeysuckle. This soft perfume dominates the cool night air. And though the air is desert dry, you can taste it: it is as heady as the finest champagne.

At ten o'clock that night, having avoided Lyel all evening so I wouldn't have to discuss Tony and Alicia Gebhardt's offer, I drove up Broadmore Road with the

truck windows rolled down, drinking in this air and
marveling at the contrast to the stench of Los Angeles
or New York. What is now New York once smelled this
sweet; L.A. once tasted of the sea. The combustion engine has changed all that. Now lakes go sterile from acid
rain. Trees die trying to breathe.

The only hole in the security fence had been caused
by the crash and led directly onto the runways, where I
might be easily noticed. I elected to take a back route. I
parked off the road, just beyond a For Sale sign, at the
edge of a twenty-acre lot with a single-story brick ranch
house in the southeast corner. This close to the airport,
they would only interest deaf people in a sale. I elected
to park and hike the quarter mile to the hangar rather
than drive into the airport's empty lot at night and
possibly attract the attention of Cousin's hired security
boys. One of the reasons I ended up in this business was
an insatiable curiosity. As a kid I took clocks apart. Now,
I wanted to see the wreckage of that plane.

At my weight and height I'm a little like the infamous
tap-dancing elephant when I try to sneak around, but
you make do with what you have. I have a lot, so I've
learned to keep it contained, to lower my center of
gravity, hold my arms against my body, take small steps
and move slowly. All of this and dark clothing help to
camouflage movement at night. I kept the north fence
between me and the ranch house, moving roughly post
to post, using the posts as minor screens. Making do
with what I had.

On the other hand, what size costs you in sneaking
around, it compensates for by making fences seem
smaller. I can go over an eight-foot chain-link fence
nearly as easily as a teenager going over a tennis net. I
was so cocky, in fact, about my abilities that I didn't test
the fence, and I soon discovered it was loosely attached
to the support posts. I made a tremendous racket com-
pleting my vault, and I heard dogs bark both at the

ranch house and somewhere over near the airport terminal. I hurried then. Dogs cannot only be a nuisance when you're sneaking around, they can be downright dangerous, depending on how they are trained. I carry some scar tissue on my calves to prove that.

I worked the airport's perimeter, coming fully around the small parking lot, cutting across the access road, and vaulting another chain-link fence to reach the tarmac. The hangar containing the remains of the crashed airplane lay just ahead. I learned how to pick locks from a man who did it for a living; I met him when I locked myself out of a rental car one time, and he knew everything there was to know about locks and locksmithing. We worked together about two weeks during the evenings. After two days I had the basics down, but individual manufacturers, both of car locks and household locks, have their peculiar quirks about them. Becoming fluent in the art of picking a lock is something that requires many hours of patient practice. Despite what television shows would have you believe, it takes at least two tools and about five minutes to unlock the simplest of mechanisms. Commercial locks are much trickier. And like firing a handgun, it is something you must practice constantly if you hope to stay up on it. I had not stayed up on my picking; it took me nearly fifteen minutes to get the lock. In breaking and entering, that's something close to eternity. The dogs continued to bark over by the terminal. The back of my shirt was soaked from nervous tension by the time the handle turned.

The hangar was cavernous, and except for the remains of the wreck, a dark spot out in the center of the huge space, empty. My eyes had adjusted somewhat to the lack of light, but this space was as dark as a tomb and required the use of my pocket-size Mag-lite. Even in rubber-sole shoes my footfalls echoed as I strode across the slab floor toward the twisted shadows of the demolished fuselage. I examined the mess as a whole. The cabin of the plane had remained mostly intact, though charred a frightful black. The wings had been repositioned roughly where they were originally attached; the fence at the end of the runway had stripped them cleanly from the fuselage. The two tines of the propeller were bent back toward the cockpit in an ugly manner, this from the nose dive the plane had done following the loss of most of the landing superstructure. The nice part for me was that because the wings had been torn off, they had not burned. Whereas much of the craft had blistered to the point of melting, the wings, though bent and structurally damaged, were otherwise as they were at the moment of impact.

The plane, a commercial chemical duster, was equipped with spray delivery apparatus along each wing. With the penlight in my mouth, I tried to find a way to loosen any of the mechanism in order to allow me access to the fluid I suspected it would still contain. Although the nozzles were clearly adjustable, even removable, the nuts securing them were so tight that it would require a wrench to move them. I roamed the area, finally finding a workbench way over on the far side of the spacious hangar and thereupon several sets of wrenches. I brought the box-end and open-end wrenches back to the wreck with me and made quick work of one of the nozzles. As fluid dripped out of the nozzle, I caught a drop on my fingertip and lifted it to my nose. Petroleum fuel, not some fertilizer or chemical, no doubt about it. I reassembled the nozzle and then went to the torn end of the wing, where I located the aluminum feed tube for the spray mechanism. It had been ripped from the fuselage, its jagged, torn mouth sharp enough to puncture the end of my finger. I was sucking on my wound when the door of the hangar opened, flooding the space with a wash of light from the parking lot. I distinctly saw two men step through the door before it was shut, one big, one skinny. A flashlight's cone of light swept close to me. I wasn't carrying my Detonics, which I immediately regretted. I have seldom fired the handgun at another individual, but it is an amazing deterrent in situations like these.

With nowhere to run, I elected to remain where I was. True, I was facing a criminal charge, but that's what lawyers are for. The two split up and approached me with a great distance between them. That worried me, because it showed experience. Only people who have been trained or people who have been hurt before take such precautions. I wasn't anxious to meet either.

Cops would have announced themselves, so I assumed these were Cousin's men. Alerted by the barking dogs, they were making the rounds.

Their faces were hard to see in the scarce light, but as they drew closer, one circling completely around me, the flashlight jerked and I thought I recognized the skinny one in front of me. As a friend of mine paraphrased once, "Familiarity breeds content." The bastardization rang true: I felt better knowing this kid was a local. Rightly or wrongly, it somehow made him seem less ominous.

Slim approached me slowly and cautiously. He was exceptionally small and weasellike, with a pinched zitty face, long eyelashes, and wet lips. He produced a .22-caliber revolver. A pea-shooter, the cops called it.

At the same time, his oversized sidekick moved behind me and placed a cool, sharp blade against my neck. He had not showered in recent memory.

"Mr. Klick," Slim addressed me in an appropriately sinister voice. "You are a stupid fuckhead."

"Somebody's got to do it," I replied, surprised he knew me by name. I thought I knew his face—in a small community you get to know nearly everyone by sight—but because of my infrequent visits, I knew very few people by name. Had I been so predictable that Cousin had alerted his security boys to my possible return? That seemed unlikely. Perhaps I had tripped an alarm.

Silence. I was not particularly keen on the silence. In point of fact, I would have welcomed a marching band right about then. "You're someplace you don't belong. That's against the law," Slim said.

"Maybe we should call the cops," I suggested.

"I don't think so."

"Just a thought."

"You got a cheap mouth on you, pal."

"Got it in a fire sale," I said. "This airplane started the fire."

The man at my back was wearing leather gloves. I could smell them over his body odor. A blade of a knife toyed with the lobe of my right ear. "You remember Vincent van Gogh, don't you, Klick?" the big one asked me from behind.

Three mistakes: the big guy who smelled bad was overly confident and was standing too close for his own good. The pea-shooter didn't particularly scare me, and was not the kind of gun a security guard would carry. The third mistake was to physically threaten me. I don't like the thought of people hurting me, and I'm willing to take about any chance to prevent it. They let me think about losing my ear, and that was stupid. I made my move.

I took hold of the hand that was toying with my ear, lowered my shoulder, tossed my hip into it, and leveraged him up, over, and squarely down onto the plane's wing. This in turn caused Slim to backpedal in order to stay clear. He stumbled into a piece of the propeller. I jumped the wing. Slim was just lifting the gun again when I took it from him. I chopped him strongly in the windpipe with the meat of my hand, grabbed hold of him by the back of his collar, and, pivoting, swung him like I would a bale of hay, releasing at the apex of my turn. No more than half my weight, he flew through the air like a wingless bird and crashed on the debris of the disemboweled aircraft. I kicked my bigger friend in the face—not the nicest way to fight, but effective. It kept him down.

Before I knew it, I was running—charging, actually—at a full head of steam through a hayfield for my truck. Somewhere back there I had vaulted the chain-link fence. Somewhere back there I heard dogs barking.

Somewhere back there were two very pissed-off people.

9

"I propose you challenge Cousin about the way he runs his security operations and give a full report to Sheriff Norton. This kind of thing shouldn't be allowed to happen."

I sucked down my drink. "I was there illegally, Lyel," I reminded him. "I'm the one who broke the law." He seemed about to say something, but I persisted. "It was a mistake, of course. They came in a few seconds too late; they didn't determine what I had seen; and they knew my name without asking. At first they struck me as professionals, but now I'm thinking amateurs. I doubt seriously they belong to the airport—so the question remains: whose amateurs?"

"I still think it's worth a mention to Norton," he said.

I didn't respond to that. Another thought had occurred.

"Something Steven said to me: he mentioned a stuntman. He didn't mean anything by it, but it got me thinking. We don't know much about this pilot, do we? I'd like to find out a little more."

"Why all the interest in the plane?"

"A man died, Lyel, under bizarre circumstances. Curiosity is one of the prerequisites in my line of work. It's not something you just turn off. You're stuck with it."

"And you're curious?"

"Very."

"But not about Roberta McGreggor?"

He had beaten me to this before I could outline my plans. "I knew you'd get around to that," I said. "Let's review Bert's case for a moment. We have the concern of a woman described as a motherly sister. We have a wildcat of a woman with cash on her hands and gambling in her heart, who is known to stray from time to time. Add to this that we have absolutely no leads indicating foul play of any sort. If I were reporting to Bruce on this case, if she were some burnt-out rock star we were after, I would tell him that the next step was to check with the drag racers out at the INEL, and then, one by one, every gambling joint in Nevada. In our line of work, unless she was a reincarnation of Janis Joplin, we wouldn't bother. Too expensive. Too much of a long shot."

"What's going on, Klick?" he asked. He knew me too well.

Reluctantly, I told him about the Gebhardt's offer. Even Lyel seemed to recognize it as a good deal, and he also seemed to appreciate a woman being involved. He was anxious to see me get over Nicole. I finished by saying: "My present plan is to spend a few days on this case, swing down to L.A. and check in with Bruce, and, while I'm at it, look into our pilot's past and see if he ever had a Hollywood career going. A few days isn't going to hurt us. The McGreggor thing is stalled."

"Wouldn't it be easier to phone his widow? Paper mentioned a widow," Lyel said.

"Are you offering to help?"

"Two conditions: one we go to the INEL: two, you tell Candice, not me. If you won't completely abandon Candice, we'll follow up when there's something to follow up. I'll keep on it while you're gone."

"I thought you'd give me a harder time."

"I like you with your ears on." He added, "A few days away might be a good thing for you."

"I didn't know you cared," I said.

"Yes you did," replied Lyel, heading back to the bar.

I was beginning to feel the drink. I felt unrealistically good. Lyel and I tended to drink to extremes. I had this nagging worry that my body could only hold a finite amount of alcohol, that when I reached a certain quantity, measured by now in hundreds—thousands?—of cocktails and beers, I would have to stop.

I bottom-upped my rum and tonic in fear that one day soon I'd have to quit.

"Thirsty?" Lyel asked, noticing this.

I tried to explain how I felt about our drinking. He nodded. He didn't agree, but he didn't try to argue. He simply nodded and poured another drink.

10

Cars coming down the long gravel lane have a distinct sound, even a half mile away. I knew someone was coming. My instincts were confirmed when Derby stopped chasing frogs and looked up toward the house. She cocked her head and ran toward the drive, her tail going like a metronome. She pranced across the lawn, leaping energetically.

I waved from my lawn chair as Candy McGreggor climbed out of a ten-year-old Chevy Nova. She wore corduroy cutoffs that, had they been scissored an inch higher, would have been crotchless. Though she was a small woman, her tan legs appeared lean and strong. Her T-shirt was two sizes too small, leaving a gap of tan skin above the corduroys, and she was braless.

"Hey there," she shouted as she navigated across the dug-up lawn. "Saw Lyel in town. He said you two were going over to Arco this afternoon, so I thought it was a good time to come clean house."

Going over the INEL had been my one major concession to Lyel. Essentially I was abandoning the case, so I wanted to stop her from cleaning my house. But to do so would have only made matters worse. In her mind she had a debt to repay.

There was something refreshing about Candy. She

was sure of herself, with none of the insecurities so many women have. She marched right over to me and slouched down into the companion lawn chair, hooking a leg over the armrest and rocking her ankle so that her flip-flop slapped her heel. "Whew! What a morning," she proclaimed. She looked around. "Pretty," she said more softly. "Real pretty."

"Sure is." I was looking at her. She was looking at the slough. It reminded me of a scene from an old Cary Grant movie. I looked out at the slough. She looked over at me. I didn't need to see her looking, I could feel it.

"Did Lyel tell you about Bert's car?" she asked.

"No." I hadn't heard from Lyel this morning. I assumed he was sleeping in.

"The car was paid off. Paid in full." She waited for my reaction. "That's an expensive car, Mr. Klick."

"Chris . . ." I said. Nick had told me that Bert had been in the chips lately. Maybe no one had told sister Candy, and so I did.

Candy jerked her head the other way.

"What can you tell me about her debts?" I asked. I didn't want to tell her I was taking a leave of absence from her case, despite my agreement with Lyel.

She chuckled sarcastically. "Bert owes *everyone* at least a little." She unhooked her leg from the arm of the chair and sat up. "Been the same way all her life. Some people just like to spend money, I guess, whether they got it or not. Funny, 'cause I don't care one way or the other. Course, I don't got it, so I never had the chance. That's the thing about money; it's kinda like booze. Know what I mean? You get kind of a tolerance for it or something. Pretty soon what you're making ain't enough. Some of the fanciest people in town bounce checks. Don't make no sense at all."

I pointed out the flickers feeding their young and she was mesmerized by the ritual. "So is there a reason why

Bert might have wanted to disappear?" I tried after a while.

"Her debts; is that what you're sayin'?" she asked. "You think she ran away?"

"Something like that. There are any number of possibilities. Someone may have offered to pay off her more important debts if she would spend some time with him in return."

She recoiled at the thought.

"She might have been too embarrassed, too confused to explain it to anyone. Especially her sister. Pack a bag and hit the road. Explain it later."

"That's Bert," she admitted. "She tends to do something and then think about it later. You've met Nick. You know what I mean. Nothin' wrong with Nick. Not really. But Bert deserves better."

"We don't know anything for sure," I reminded her.

"The more we find out, the less I want to know."

I nodded. Nothing new there. "One of the pitfalls of this kind of work, you spend your time turning over stones. It's usually dark, damp, and dirty under stones."

"You're giving up, ain't you?" She tried to sound disappointed, but it was a voice of acceptance. I didn't answer. "Where do you want me to start?" she asked, standing in front of me, innocent and yet beguiling. Sunlight caught the side of her face.

I heard a car arriving. "Anywhere. It could use a woman's touch." The car pulled in and stopped.

"Hello there!" Alicia called from the drive. She looked like something from a fashion layout. "Down, down," she said as Derby sought affection.

"Who's that?" Candy said in a suspicious voice.

"Hi," I hollered over to Alicia. "Just met her the other day," I said to Candy.

"Lucky her," Candy said, suddenly in no hurry to start with the cleaning.

Alicia jumped carefully over the small trenches,

Derby nipping at the heels of her white sandals. I introduced the two women.

"Do you work here?" Alicia said, somewhat cattily.

"I'm paying back a favor," replied Candy. She turned
to me, "I'll clean the bedroom first, Chris." She walked
off before I could respond.

Alicia raised her eyebrows. "Am I interrupting?"

"Have a seat." I stood and started after Candy.
"Something to drink? Beer, iced tea, soda?" I asked over
my shoulder.

"Beer," Alicia called out after me.

"It's not like that," I explained to Candy at the door. I
had no idea why I felt compelled to defend myself.

She held the door for me. "Oh, really?" she said suspiciously.

I headed to the refrigerator.

"By the way," she asked. "Where *is* the bedroom?"

11

I joined back up with Alicia, delivering the beer. Her blouse was sheer salmon-colored silk. She wore white linen shorts that were fashionably baggy. They were cinched at the waist by a belt made of lizard hide. The buckle was gold. Her long nails were manicured in the French style, the underside of the tips colored a soft creamy white, a clear gloss applied to the surface. She wore a Rolex watch with a platinum and gold band, the face encrusted with diamonds. When the wind blew my way I was teased by a hint of a fragrance so sweet I actually closed my eyes and drank it in.

She asked me about the yard, and I told her about my ongoing sprinkler installation.

"So," I said after a short silence.

"So why haven't I heard from you?"

"It's only been one day," I said.

"I'm impatient."

"So I gather."

"If you don't want to tell me, that's fine." She glanced in the direction of the cabin. Toward Candy. "Perhaps there were other things on your . . . mind." The deliberate pause elicited the desired effect: I blushed.

"I've thought about your offer," I told her.

"That's good." She leaned forward. The silk slithered

over the tops of her breasts like river water over smooth stone. "And?"

"I would have to leave immediately?" I inquired.

"We would. Yes. Tomorrow." She searched my eyes. "I feel I should be on the scene. Any objection to that?"

"I suppose not."

"You don't have to sound so thrilled."

I heard a car in the distance. I assumed it was Lyel, on schedule, driving the dune buggy I kept stored in his four-car garage. Lucille is the Columbo of cars. An off-road vehicle, her exterior is pitted, scraped, and mended from several full rolls, a number of collisions with natural objects, and long hard rallies in the harshest elements. But beneath her is a Porsche engine, rack-and-pinion steering, and the best German-engineered suspension money can buy. She is very fast off the line and can push one-twenty on the straightaway.

The only extraneous piece of equipment in her stripped interior is a Sony car stereo with forty watts of added power and two full-range speakers. Most people elect to leave off the extremely vulnerable muffler, but I'm not fond of loud rally cars, and so Lucille has been retro-fitted with a rear-mounted stack muffler I scavenged from a junkyard Peterbilt. She hums instead of screams. I've never liked screamers.

The car arrived, but it wasn't Lyel. It was our neighbor Julie and her toddler, Jill. Derby charged. I whistled to stop her, but it did no good. She attacked Jill playfully, knocking her down. Jill screamed, in tears, and kicked Derby viciously. I shouted for Jill to stop, and Jill cried all the louder. Alicia was up and right behind me.

"You don't have to yell at her!" Alicia scolded me, helping Jill. Both Alicia and Julie glared at me.

"She kicked the dog in the face," I said in self-defense.

"Your dog practically killed the child," Alicia said.

Jill let out an ear-shattering scream as Darby attempted to lick her.

"Julie," I said too harshly, "can't you *do* something?"

"Chris, it's your dog," Candy scolded, jumping off the deck.

"She's just a baby," Alicia reminded me. All three women were comforting Jill. On cue they all looked up and gave me the hairy eyeball. I was being driven from my own home. Then I realized they wanted me to call Derby. She was licking Jill's neck again, and Jill didn't appreciate it.

I whistled. Derby didn't come. I called her name. She didn't come.

"*You* do something," Julie demanded.

"Chris!" Alicia echoed.

Lucille pulled to a stop, Lyel at the wheel. The cavalry. I waved and ran full speed toward the car, leaping the sprinkler trenches effortlessly. The women were all calling my name, nearly in unison. Derby was still licking Jill's face, tail wagging.

"They'll figure it out," I told a dumbfounded Lyel.

"Beg your pardon?" he said, looking back and forth between the three women and myself.

"Lay rubber," I ordered.

He put his foot to the floor and we were gone in two plumes of dust. That's what friends are for.

12

We switched seats in Ridland, and I drove for nearly two hours through the towns of Picabo and Carey, past the Craters of the Moon and into Arco. We passed an enormous sign announcing we had entered the INEL. Heat rising from the desert floor distorted the distant mountains and made eerie the boxlike nuclear reactors all around us. The unforgiving sun had worked the sign's blue paint into dragon scales. A quarter mile ahead the road turned left, the highway edging the western border of the ten-square-mile government site rather than running through it. We passed a number of road signs warning us that trespass was forbidden. In the distant parking lots, the hundreds of buses used to transport the ten thousand workers required to keep the fifty-four reactors running were lined up like toys.

I slowed down. We passed a souped-up primer-colored Camaro parked in the breakdown lane: fat rear rubber, jacked-up back end, twin fiberglass scoops on the hood, and an antenna springed and curved from front bumper to back. A boy about fifteen could be seen behind the wheel. He held a burning cigarette between clenched teeth and twisted lips, his eyes squinting to see through the blue vapor trail.

"We're here," Lyel informed me. "The car we passed was the scout on this end."

"Yes."

If we were the cops, he would send out a code over the CB radio. If not, he would send out a different code that warned the racers up ahead that the availability of two lanes would soon be restricted. Except for aerial patrols, it made busting them damn near impossible.

There were eleven cars in all. They were pulled off to the side of the road, kids leaning on their hoods in white T-shirts and moussed hairdos, wearing blue jeans, and listening to Eddie Van Halen. Most were smoking cigarettes. The rest were chewing gum. I pulled off the road. A cloud of dust from the road's shoulder rolled up over Lucille, momentarily obscuring the group.

Next to these kids, Lyel and I looked like the twin towers of the World Trade Center looming over Wall Street. But whereas Lyel looked distinctly L.L. Bean, I was shirtless, wearing only running shorts and Nike Air Jordans. We were, as always, an odd pair.

"How you doing?" Lyel asked the one closest to us. He had bad skin, and his arms were suntanned the color of ten-year-old cowhide. He couldn't have been a day over seventeen. He looked to be the oldest.

He nodded, took a drag on his cigarette, and said, "We ain't doing nothing wrong."

I scratched my balls. Tough guys always scratch their balls. "You aren't racing? We were hoping—"

"What'd you have in mind?" the kid asked.

I said loudly, "About ninety-five for two miles. I guess I heard wrong. Twenty bills says there's not a car out here that can dust mine."

The kid smiled. "What do you got under that piece of shit?" he asked.

"Horsepower," I replied.

"Two miles?" the other asked. "We usually do a half mile or a mile."

"Whatever," I replied in a deep voice. "My Lucille likes two."

"Twenty bucks. You really want to race that thing?"

"I really do," I replied.

"It's not exactly fair," he said confidently.

I smiled. "We'll see," I said, knowing he was right. A dune buggy is not a dragster. The boy nodded and climbed into his car through the window. When he started it up I thought one of the nuclear reactors had exploded. "You stay here," I told Lyel, as if we hadn't worked this out in advance. I scratched my balls again. He nodded. He would ask around about Bert McGreggor while I raced. Then we would switch roles.

There is an intriguing excitement generated from behind the steering wheel moments before a race, an unparalleled adrenaline rush. I have felt the same thing before a fight: fear mixed with uncertainty and possibility. A front tire going flat at these speeds can kill you. The other car, improperly handled, can kill you. I was accustomed to rallies and cross-country races, which require different skills than a drag contest. There is finesse required in off-road racing; drag racing requires nerves of steel, steady arms, perfect gear work, and a heavy foot. The Camaro and I taxied up to our starting positions. A boy stood on the pavement in front of us, a small flag in each hand. The Camaro roared as the young driver cleaned out his valves.

Lucille purred. I fastened the other half of my cross-shouldered fixed–seat-belt system and set the seat back a few inches more to allow me to lock my elbows. I didn't expect to end up twenty dollars richer, but I wanted to give a good chase; there was no telling where this Camaro fit into the pack. It could have been the fastest car or the slowest. If I gave a poor showing they would shun us. I needed to buy Lyel some time to ask around about Bert. To drive two hours for a one-minute race was not my idea of an efficient use of time. The starter waited for a thumbs-up from each of us. The flags fell. I eased out the clutch and pushed my right foot to the floor.

The Camaro lurched ahead, as I had expected. Its horsepower proved overwhelming. That was why I had hoped for a two-mile race: he had the raw horsepower, but my Lucille was not slow by any means and was custom-geared for rallies, with both a superlow gear for hill climbing and an amazingly high overdrive for the flats. The overdrive conserved fuel and generated outrageous land speeds. But the speed came at a cost; the drawback was that she was so highly geared she lacked power. I would need distance and perfect gear work to beat something like this Camaro.

Kids like these tended to drive each gear to a high RPM before shifting. It sounds good, but it is an inefficient use of the system. I knew Lucille inside out. Shifting her was a matter of smooth timing and great finesse. While Mr. Camaro roared through his, I knew I might beat him by working Lucille through a steady set of four. I watched him pull away as I moved the stick through second and into third. Then I began to close the distance. I pulled even with his rear bumper as I slapped her into fourth. He jumped ahead just before his next shift, but as his exhaust belched in the change, I charged ahead, my arms extended, eyes wide, the wheel shaking. Even with the Peterbilt stack, she was complaining. With her Porsche engine, Lucille was hot enough, willing enough, to blow herself apart for me. I had no desire to kill her racing a zit-faced teenager, but I kept my foot down, and she zipped ahead of the Camaro. Ninety-seven miles per hour.

The Camaro caught back up, coming alongside. At a buck five he glanced over at me. I saw it out of the corner of my eye. It was an amateurish move. One moment, there he was; the next, he was off the road, disappearing in a cloud of desert dust.

I crossed the finish line alone.

On my way back I saw the problem: fresh road kill. A flattened prairie dog. Having glanced in my direction, he had spotted the animal too late, had twitched at the wheel and had thrown himself off the road.

I motored back to the pack of kids, triumphant, and requested we stretch the course to two miles, treating it something like dealer's choice in poker. Lyel nodded at me with that prehistoric sunken-eye stare of his that told me he was getting somewhere. No one challenged my right to adjust the course. The far scout was positioned another mile out, and a second opponent took the lane beside Lucille. Another Chevy, she was an older model, gunmetal gray, with oversize slicks on the rear, some serious springs in the back, and a turbocharger cut into the hood. She was all engine. Evil. The boy behind the wheel looked like Dennis the Menace without the freckles.

My hands on the wheel were sticky with sweat. Inside Lucille, I felt like an ant trapped in a rusty old tin can. The blacktop disappeared in shimmering silver heat waves. It looked like the road ran into a windblown lake of sand and tinsel.

I was better with the gears on this second go-round, fluid. The Chevy sucked past me early, but Lucille won. When we returned to the pits the driver of the Chevy consulted one of the older ones, a boy-man who appeared to be in charge. The boy-man said, "What about your buddy?"

"He doesn't race."

"Sixty bucks says he does," the kid challenged.

Lyel approached me and murmured in my ear, "It's a hustle." We walked away from the group.

"Damn right," I agreed. "I think that Chevy could have sucked me up her tubes."

"What do you think? You mind?"

"I think you race Lucille and I talk to the gearheads. We're up forty. Who cares if we lose a little?"

"My feelings exactly," he agreed.

"How are we doing out here?"

"Guy you want to talk to is in the back there with the thick brow." Lyel was not one to talk about thick brows.

I nodded. "Lucille can probably beat that one, Lyel," I assured him when I saw the Dodge Charger wheel out onto the blacktop. "Drop into gears earlier than you think. Have patience. I think they're trying to suck us in deeper. The car to watch is that Buick. That and the Firebird. You can beat this Charger hands down."

"Earlier than I think," he repeated.

"Patience," I reminded him.

Lyel climbed in and pulled Lucille alongside the Charger. It seemed like everyone but me was smoking a cigarette. The flag fell, the tires spun, and the cars disappeared down the stretch in a cloud of foul-smelling gray smoke. I wiped my hands on my sweaty chest and moved toward the kid Lyel had pointed out.

I wandered among the cars, pretending to admire them. The kid with thick fingers and a bulging brow picked up on me, following me closely with his eyes. As I neared, he asked, "He any good?"

"Very." Eddie Van Halen ended. Someone put on a U2 tape. It blared out across the flats.

"You know a gal named Bert from over in Butte Peak?" I asked.

Thick Head thought about this. I inspected the rear suspension on an older-model Ford. It was lifted a foot higher than a factory issue. Big rubber. Aluminum mag wheels. The raised rear aimed the front grill toward the road so that it looked like Derby stretching after a long nap. "Bert," I repeated, in case Thick Head had thick ears. "She drives a red Mustang."

"What about her?" the guy asked.

I watched his reflection in the hubcap. He looked

over the roof of the car at someone, and it seemed to me
it was for some kind of approval. "Red Mustang," I said
again, turning to look at him.

He looked back at me too quickly. I rose and looked at
the guy on the other side of the car, the guy he'd been
looking at. He was a farmer's-son type: overalls,
freckles, a wad of gum exercising his jaw. Junior. He had
green eyes, and they were locked onto mine. If Thick
Head was afraid of me, this kid wasn't, despite my size.
"How 'bout you?" I asked. "Know who I'm talking
about?"

"Sure do," he said. He had a sixteen-year-old's broken
voice. Not quite a man, not quite a kid. "Haven't seen
Bert in a couple weeks."

"Is that right?"

He nodded.

"I heard she drives a hot car," I said.

"For a cunt, she ain't bad. You guys come to race or
talk?" A couple of the other boys laughed.

For a moment I sensed something sinister. Were these
kids dangerous enough to have hurt Bert—to have
robbed or raped her, killed her, and then hidden her
body and the car?

The sound of the CB radio crackling caught our attention. One of the kids stuck his head inside the car. When
he pulled it out he said, "The old guy won."

I smiled at Junior. "We came to race."

I edged around the Chevy, passed Junior and his Eldorado, and reached a fairly new Pontiac Firebird. The
owner said, "I know who you're talking about."

"Is that right?"

"Baxter's pissed off because Bert's beat him the last
two times out."

"Mechanical problems," Junior Baxter hollered, over-
hearing. "The bitch just got lucky, that's all." Maybe
someone like Baxter had killed her all by himself.

"She's taken some money off of all of us. What about her?"

"I hear it's a nice car," I said.

"Pretty standard. Nick's done a couple things to it. With all the extras, it comes off the line pretty hot to begin with. He didn't have to do much."

Lyel and the Charger returned. Lyel hung a U-turn and waited at the line. "Who's next?" he yelled out over the noise of his vanquished opponent's engine.

"I'll go," shouted Thick Head. But the others laughed.

"I'm next," said Junior Baxter. He got in his Eldorado and started the engine. If there was a muffler on it, there was no packing inside. A minute later the tires squealed and the cars disappeared down the blacktop. Lyel had an early edge, but Baxter suddenly shot out in front, leaving him well behind.

I asked the agreeable one with the Pontiac, "when was the last time you saw Bert?"

He thought for a moment. "Last time I saw Bert was two weeks ago. I remember because she knows when most of us get paid, and that woman likes to bet." He repeated himself. "Two weeks ago Friday. I lost fifty to her, I oughta remember that."

"Nick with her?"

"No. She got so she come out here by herself. Wednesday and Friday nights, all day Saturday are race days. She was really throwing the money around last time she was out."

"I heard she never has a cent."

"Hey, how would I know? All I know is that she was waving some big bucks around last time she was out here. Challenged anyone here to a hundred-dollar race. Said she was celebrating."

"Anyone take her up on it?"

"You kidding? Hey, listen. Most of the time we race for the fun of it. Costs enough just keeping gas in your car. People like Bert, people like you guys, they hear about us and want to race. Put some money up. That's okay. Sometimes you make, sometimes you break, right? But it's nothing regular with us. This is kind of a club, you know? No one wants to hose the other guy. The idea is to dink around with your wheels and see if you can't shave a few seconds off last week's time. We don't do much side-by-side. Most of it's clock work." He lit a cigarette.

"You gonna race?" I asked.

He whispered, "You want to save some money? Go home. You know what's going down?" He didn't wait for my reply. "You and your friend is getting hustled."

"Why tell me?"

"I don't go for side-by-side. Soon as you get out of here, we can go back to the clock." He looked at his watch. "I got to be at the station in twenty minutes. Means I won't get a run today, if you and your friend stick around."

"I'll keep that in mind," I said. "And thanks."

He sucked on his cigarette.

Lyel lost the next three races; a hundred and fifty bucks. Petty cash for him. I climbed in behind the driver's seat for the ride home. "We got what we came for," I said. "Bert has burned a couple of guys here. Maybe one too many times, but I don't think so. Two weeks ago Friday, she was over here waving money around. Said she was celebrating."

"Friday night?" Lyel said. "But we know Candice and Nick saw her that weekend."

"Exactly right."

"So the involvement of these guys seems unlikely. Possible, but unlikely," Lyel said.

"Which means we've exhausted the most likely possibilities."

"You don't sound completely convinced. I thought you would try justifying your trip to California again."

"It's only for a few days," I said. "Maybe less, unless there's a reason to stay."

"You have something else you're thinking about, Klick?" he asked, throwing it back to me.

There was something else. But I had no desire to bring it up.

Lyel waved. The kids ignored us. "God that was fun," he said. If he said anything else I missed it; a car behind us took off from the line and I wouldn't have heard if he'd yelled in my ear.

13

Candy McGreggor lived in Woodside, a housing development on the southeastern fringe of Butte Peak, not far from her sister's duplex. It was a somewhat congested, mixed development, part condo, part single-family residence, just north of the sewer treatment plant and just south of an indoor tennis facility. A squadron of kids on bikes with banana seats raced past my truck. One about eight years old jerked his bike into a wheelie and led the pack up a bike path that weaved through the surrounding fields of sage and waxwood balsam. Two dogs followed the kids, barking nearly in unison.

Derby, who had insisted on joining me in the cab of my pickup, started to bark back but stopped as I turned to scold her. She jumped across my lap and threw her head out the window, blocking my vision. I ordered her to sit, pushing her back and nearly driving off the road.

I left Derby in the cab. Candy's house, a rental, no doubt, had a For Sale sign on the front lawn. I climbed the concrete front steps and rang a glowing door bell.

"Come in!" she hollered.

The small living room was clean and simple. I could smell chocolate chip cookies baking. She offered me a beer, but I declined. The furniture in the room was arranged around the television and stereo. The VCR looked well used.

Candy wore tight faded blue jeans, no belt, no shoes, and a two-tone blue T-shirt that read CLOSE FLAP BEFORE STRIKING. She turned around and I read DIAMOND—A GIRL'S BEST FRIEND, with a blowup of a strike-anywhere match. She must have used a shoe horn to get herself into the jeans. I sat at the kitchen table while she made some coffee. The Twin Falls *Times-News* was open to Dear Abby.

She had no pretense whatsoever. I felt as if I had been living with her for a couple of years. She was the quintessential opposite of Alicia Gebhardt, flawed, but not without redeeming assets. It occurred to me then, as it had so often lately, that I was repeatedly attracted to the wrong kind of woman. Candy would be loyal, funny, considerate, and, I had a hunch, somewhat wild in bed. Everything I was looking for. I had a feeling that after a week or so I wouldn't see the misuse of makeup, wouldn't hear the abuse of the language. All I would need was a La-Z-Boy recliner and a Rotary membership.

"So, what's up?" she asked, filling the Mr. Coffee with cold water.

"You did a great job on my house."

"Thanks."

"I mean it. The flowers were a nice touch."

"A man shouldn't live alone. A man don't know anything about keeping up a place, making it liveable."

It sounded like an invitation. I sat there for a while, enjoying the peace of the place. She had created a home here; it felt right.

"Something occurred to me," I said. "About Bert. What about her job?"

She nodded, putting a plate of the freshly baked cookies on the table. "You're thinking she stumbled across something at City Hall." She said it in such a way that I knew she'd been thinking the same thing. "She could have gotten herself in trouble and taken off, afraid to admit what she'd done."

"Could it happen?" I asked.

"You mean could she have been mixed up in something illegal? *Of course* it could happen! Voter registrations, land deeds, devalued land assessment, tax fraud. Companies, partnerships, you name it. It all goes through City Hall. There's only eleven of us that work in the whole building! We all see *everything*. Butte Peak is the county seat. Every piece of business from Snow Lake to Hill City goes through our office."

"Can you get me in there?" I asked.

"No way. There are all sorts of laws against that. It could mean major trouble. But *I* could look into it. I know what to look for. Nothing illegal about me doing it, either. Be easier if I had a specific date or a name or something."

"She paid off the car loan a couple weeks ago. I'd start there."

Candy said, "Sure. I can do that."

"I didn't mean *you*, exactly. It could be dangerous."

Her face paled. "You think she sold information?"

She could see the answer in my face. "I'd rather check City Hall myself," I said.

After a long, thoughtful pause, she said, "No. It should be me. I work there. I'll just stay a little late, that's all. It's no problem. I have every right to poke around in my sister's desk."

"It might be better if I do it," I tried again.

"No, sir," she said. "I'm telling you, this is completely cool if I do it." She paused. "Something tells me this is not exactly a new idea for you."

"The idea nagged at me the minute one of her co-workers described the kind of work they do," I explained. "But at the time . . . it's just that you want to exhaust all of the most likely possibilities before you go breaking into City Hall—which is what I had planned. When a lot of money was mentioned—and it came up again today out at the INEL—I had to look more seriously at where that money might have come from. Gambling is certainly a possibility. It's one explanation."

"But so is slipping someone information from City Hall," she said.

"The point being, this is where things can get dirty."

"You needed to prepare me for this," she said, realizing that without seeing other possibilities fail, she might not have given this one a chance.

I shrugged. Destroying idols, if it came to that, was not my idea of fun. I told her I had to leave town for a couple of days, but she appeared preoccupied and seemed not to be bothered by the announcement. She seemed sad. I wanted to hold her in my arms and comfort her.

I was saved by the ringing of the phone. Candy answered it, and five minutes into her conversation I kissed her on the cheek and left.

She waved good-bye, her eyes begging me to stay.

14

San Francisco is one of my favorite cities. It maintains a charm that still manages to resist the urban mega-city feel that dominates New York and Los Angeles. When I'm in town by myself I normally stay at the Obrero, a Basque bed-and-breakfast in Chinatown. Alicia selected the St. Francis. We requested two nonadjoining rooms. I got a terrific night of sleep.

In the morning, we drove by the property she was interested in. It was an ordinary-looking warehouse in a commercial zone south of Redwood City.

We then started in City Hall, as any self-respecting investigator would. It took ninety minutes to find out the property was owned by a company called Pacific Rim Leasing. Simple enough. The clerk wouldn't give me any more pertinent information, like address or phone number. I asked the clerk how many other people had been in to check on the property recently. She didn't remember. She struck me as the kind of person who wouldn't remember what she had eaten that morning. Maybe she remembered what she'd smoked: Maui Zowie.

Alicia headed off in the rental car for Stanford University's business library to research Pacific Rim Leasing. I

waited at City Hall in an uncomfortable chair and read
USA Today until the clerk took a coffee break.

When Miss Maui Zowie took her break, I tried again.
This time I used my all-appealing wit, charm, and savoir
faire with a woman in her early fifties. She was a balloon
smuggler—Dolly Parton's sister. She stared back at me
as if I were a brick wall. So much for all-appealing. I
asked if there was any way to tell whether or not the
property taxes had been paid on a piece of commercial
property that my company, Pacific Rim Leasing,
owned. Our accountant had recently been caught with
his finger in the till, I explained, and we were busy
checking what had and had not been paid. I would need
a photocopy of anything she could find. "You know how
lawyers are," I said. For a brief moment she hesitated, so
I added, "I called, but I got hung up on three times."
She smirked, nodded, and said she'd look into it. Would I
take a seat please?

While she was gone I had time to marvel at the inepti-
tude of government agencies. In the computer age, tax
information should be available at the touch of a finger.
Thirty-six minutes passed before she waved me over to
the counter. I drew a volley of angry and envious looks
from the variety of people waiting in line.

"Could I see some ID please? And I'll need you to
sign."

Before the government cracked down on it, ob-
taining an alternate ID was easy: you searched public
records for an infant fatality—someone the same race
and sex who'd been born the same year you were. With
this name in hand, you retrieved a copy of the legal
birth certificate, and with a notarized birth certificate,
other documents—social security card, passport, driver's license—fell effortlessly into place. So it was that I
had two other complete identities available to me for
just such situations, one of which I had with me. I carried two wallets, to keep my selves separate. I showed

the clerk my Kenneth Carlson ID. Raleigh, North Carolina.

She printed my name. I signed below.

"No problem with our office," she said. She handed me a photocopy of a computer printout that confirmed the taxes had been paid on time. I asked her about several of the columns. The third over was the check number. The fourth was the interbank number of the issuing bank. I thanked her and returned to my seat.

When she returned, Alicia seemed simultaneously excited and disappointed. She said, "In a little over three hours we're further along than the first guy ever got. How do you explain that?"

"When you hire an investigator long distance, he'll usually take you to the cleaners. That's one reason I don't hire out. So what'd you find out?"

"Pacific Rim Leasing is owned in partnership by three other companies, Alpha Investments, Alderman Associates, and something called South Regional Development Corporation. The address is a post office box in a city branch, and the phone number was disconnected. Nothin' else I could find out about Pacific without talking to the company itself."

"And the others?"

"Even less." This was obviously the source of her disappointment. "None of the other companies was listed in any of the standard references. I suspect they are all out-of-state concerns, or even offshore, which makes them more difficult to trace."

"When and if we find those three, there will be three owners for each of them, and again, all in different states. Legal but baffling, unless you're a professional paper chaser." I had run into similar problems in the past. When people don't want to be found, it's hard to find them.

"We could check in Sacramento," she said. "Those companies have to be on record somewhere."

"True. But it could just as easily be Singapore as Sacramento."

"You have another idea."

"I have a partner," I told her.

"Lyel?"

"No. An attorney. Bruce Warren. One of the best paper chasers in the business. Spends all his time chasing royalty money owed to musicians who have names you don't remember."

"Partner?"

"My job. I told you: I spend most of my time chasing the musicians. Bruce chases the money."

"Will he help?"

"Will you pay? Bruce's efforts don't come cheap."

"I'll pay."

"I'll call."

* * *

Bruce agreed to hunt down the three companies for me. I warned him that there could be people who didn't want such searches taking place. He and I had been doing this sort of thing for several years. The music business is infested with criminals and criminal behavior, especially in the lower levels. One learns to take certain precautions, like using false names, making double-operator long-distance phone calls, and utilizing out-of-town mail drops—the kinds of things Pacific Rim Leasing was probably doing.

Bruce doesn't work quickly; I learned that long ago. He takes everything step by step, in a logical progression. His quirk is that he refuses to do a piece of business twice, refuses to repeat himself because it costs him time and money, and he doesn't like that. So, unlike me, he never gets ahead of himself. He is content to sit on lead A until lead A pays off. It's my tendency to jump to lead F or G and see if I can force any shortcuts. My way of thinking has cost me some broken ribs, several scars, and a half dozen concussions.

On our way back up to the city Alicia suddenly asked, "Why are you doing it?"

"How's that?"

"Candy McGreggor. Why are you doing it? You said there's no pay."

I glanced over at her, trying to conceal my astonishment at the question. I'd said I was working on something else, but I hadn't thought I'd told her who for. Perhaps I had. "No pay," I agreed.

"Then why?"

"I'm just a swell guy," I said.

"The *real* reason."

"I don't like fear. If people approach me with honest fear in their eyes and ask for help, I'm a sucker."

"How noble."

I looked at her suspiciously.

"It's refreshing," she said.

We rode in silence for a while. "Have you ever done any acting?" I asked.

She gave me a sideways glance of disapproval. "Meaning?"

"I have an idea, that's all."

"I'm all ears."

"Hardly," I said, eyeing her.

We returned to our respective rooms at the St. Francis and changed into professionals-at-work clothing. I wore a buttondown and tie, khakis, and a sport jacket, not my favorite attire. Alicia wore linen, silk, and Italian leather.

It took a single phone call to trace the interbank transit code for the check used to pay the property taxes on the warehouse. That gave me the name of the bank. The phone book gave me an address. The branch was in a yuppie neighborhood. Art deco neon signs advertising the likes of Patti's Premiere Pasta Palace and the

Greenback Pub. Young professionals milled about in oversize Esprit apparel carrying briefcases sold by The Sharper Image. Lots of money in this new generation— of which I was a member—but little knowledge, little experience. A frightening combination.

The interior of the bank was an overwhelming gray. The floor was white and black parquet, like a giant chessboard. There were some large potted ficus trees that helped break the gray. On closer inspection, they turned out to be silk. I was astonished at the quality of the craftsmanship. If I'd been a dog, the plastic bark might already have been wet.

As hard as I might try, I could probably never pass as a numbers type. Alicia was perfect. She looked the part. She explained what she needed to a woman in a navy blue suit who wore horn-rimmed glasses. The woman went and conferred with another woman, who disappeared through a door. "Who's he?" Miss Navy inquired as she returned to us.

I grinned at her. She seemed frightened of me. My boyish charm needed some work.

Alicia glanced at me. "Security," she said calmly. "There have been threats."

We waited for about fifteen minutes. Then the woman Navy had spoken to reappeared and ushered us through the door. We passed through a long open area where a half dozen secretaries pounded out letters on IBMs, the auto-spell functions bleeping now and again.

The small office cubicle was also done in gray. Surprise. Mr. Richard Kruger, as he introduced himself, was in his early thirties. He had reddish-brown hair, freckles, brown eyes, and thick red lips. When he talked, his teeth whistled.

"You're with accounts?" Alicia asked.

"In a bank we're all with accounts." He smiled for us. Practiced. He glanced at me briefly. I didn't smile. It wasn't part of my role. "Security," Alicia explained and motioned for me to sit down. The chair was small. I sat in the corner beneath an Ansel Adams of Yosemite.

"You understand that this requires the utmost discretion on your part," she began.

"Confidentiality is something we pride ourselves on," Kruger replied.

Alicia nodded. "No one knows about this. No one. This is merely a preliminary investigation, which is why I was hired from the private sector, rather than involving the police or other law enforcement agencies."

"I understand."

"The point is that Pacific Rim is convinced they are the victims of an embezzlement scheme, and tipping their hand at this point could give whoever is involved the chance to obscure the trail, as it were. My initial investigation is merely to determine if a certain party under suspicion could be responsible for the various forgeries. I'm sure you will understand, therefore, that it is impossible to show you the signature at this time. The legal ramifications of implicating an innocent party could negate the remainder of the investigation."

I was impressed. My earlier concern about whether or not she could act had vanished. She had me convinced. She had Mr. Richard Kruger convinced. He nodded enthusiastically. Kruger was male: it was difficult not to be carried away by her.

Because Alicia had clued Miss Navy in to the nature of our visit, a younger secretary arrived shortly with a folder containing the vitals on the Pacific Rim account.

Alicia said properly, "There's no need for me to see anything more than the signature card."

Kruger searched the folder. He was about to hand her the card when he reconsidered. "But if you're working with Pacific Rim," he said slowly, "then surely they've supplied you with the valid signatures." Alicia nearly had the card between her fingers, but Kruger pulled it back. He glanced over at me. I stared at him.

Alicia said, "All right, Mr. Kruger. You drive a hard bargain. We're not with Pacific Rim, or of course we could get the signatures from them. Exactly who we're with, I'm not permitted to tell you. But it's in the interest of the country, in the interest of a drug-free society, if you will, that I see that signature card." She glowed with sincerity. Kruger was captivated. If hers wasn't an honest face, then what was?

"The DEA?" he asked.

"You didn't hear that from me," she said.

"Nor me," I added.

"I didn't really take you for a security type," he said to me proudly.

"No," I agreed, offering my best bitten-back FBI smile.

He handed her the card. I offered her a folded piece of paper, which was supposed to carry the comparison signature. She studied both, clucked her tongue, and waved the card at me. I stood and glanced over her shoulder. It offered the same bogus address we already had. However, there were two signatures on the card, cosigners, a Jason R. Hanright and a Michael L. Tooley.

"I'll be damned," I said.

"Does that help you?" Kruger asked.

"Very much," she replied.

"Would you like a copy?" he asked.

"Thanks," I said in a low voice.

* * *

" 'You didn't hear that from me'?" I said as we reached the street. "Do you know how many laws you just violated?"

"*We* violated," she said, walking proud. "How'd I do?"

"Terrific," I proclaimed.

"Where are we headed?" she asked. "To a phone book," she answered herself, reaching a phone booth.

Both phone books had been torn from their protective cases. She offered me a disappointed look, and her eyes searched the street for another phone. But I had her cornered against the phones, and I didn't want to let her go.

"You were absolutely terrific in there," I repeated in a softer, gentler voice.

"Glad you liked it." She placed her hand on my shoulder.

"Really good. I mean it."

"Women learn how to act at a very early age. At least, this woman did. 'Smile, curtsy, say hello, dear.' We all spend a lot of our lives acting, don't you think?"

"A pitfall of modern living," I agreed. "We're taught to pretend. Self-expression is reduced to a safe zone." I bent down and kissed her on the mouth.

"Go for it, man," some wisecracking youth said from behind me.

Alicia laughed. Her hand remained on my shoulder. "Ah, city life. Ain't it grand?"

I glanced over my shoulder at the passing youth. He was wearing black leather pants and a black vest and had spiked dog collars strapped to both wrists. His hair stuck up as if he had recently flirted with several thousand volts of straight current.

"To the hotel?" I asked. I wasn't sure where it had come from, but I wasn't going to take it back.

She wrapped an arm around my waist, and we headed toward the car.

* * *

She was deep in thought as the elevator tolled out the floors. I feared she was about to turn me down. I wasn't well prepared for rejection. The doors slid open and we stepped out. Her room was to the left, mine to the right.

There was a moment of awkwardness as we both stood there. Her soft fingertips tugged at my hand. If I resisted, her hand would pull free and she would walk away. But I didn't resist.

15

She left me sitting on the edge of her bed and went to pull the curtains shut, leaving the room in a darkened haze. Then she disappeared into the bathroom. I leaned over and turned on the FM radio to hear a deep voice extolling the benefits of owning an Audi. Had to be a classical station. A moment later Vivaldi filled the room.

The great care she took saved me. It had been a long time, and I required a gentle, slow approach. Her busy fingers worked on the knots in my back and lower legs. Ten fingers bringing me back from my months of monkhood. Somewhere along the way I lost my bearings.

A layer of perspiration had formed between us. We had rolled over at some point. Her legs were hooked firmly around mine. Our skin made smacking and sucking noises.

An ad for sugarless peppermint gum brought us back. We laughed. Somewhere in the distance a jet took off. She kissed me. We rolled up in the bedspread, wrapped together.

After a half hour or so, she uncoiled herself and rose to stand naked before me. "I'll call Hanright and Tooley and book us appointments for tomorrow. Too late to expect to see them today. Let's have room service send up a couple drinks and find some old movie on the tube. Then, you know. Whatever happens. What do you say?"

"I say skip the phone calls, skip the drinks, skip the movie. But that last part, about things happening? Things are happening right now."

With that, she dived back into bed.

* * *

The law offices of Hanright, McElvine, Smolkowski & Paterson occupied a corner of the fifteenth floor, with a view overlooking the Golden Gate Bridge. Since he had been a signatory on Pacific Rim's bank account and since Pacific Rim owned the warehouse, he was my best lead. The waiting room was windowless and done in American Attorney: wood-paneled walls, an assortment of glossy outdoor magazines, *Scientific American,* and law journals. Jason R. Hanright's office was somewhere on the other side of the mahogany door to the right of the mahogany desk occupied by the woman with mahogany hair. I figured the receptionist had most likely been chosen for her hair color. The phone rang every few minutes, and she answered by announcing all four names in a cadence that made them incomprehensible.

Thirty minutes passed before the door opened and a soft, pale man in his mid-fifties wearing a blue suit and bifocals waved me over. He shook my hand and led me to his office.

Hanright had the look of a heart disease candidate. His breathing was awkward and he was overweight. The coffeepot behind him was three quarters empty and there were two candy wrappers in his trash can. Chocolate and creamy caramel.

He wheezed any word with an *h* in it. "Hhhow can I hhhelp you?" he asked.

I explained, "I'm investigating ownership of a warehouse here in town. The warehouse is owned by a com-

pany called Pacific Rim Leasing. You and a Mr. Michael
L. Tooley are signatories to the Pacific Rim bank account. For this reason I presume you can put me in
touch with the legal owners of the warehouse."

Attorneys are much too practiced. He smiled, very
much in control. The smile stayed in place for several
seconds. "Is this a joke?" he asked.

I assured him it was not.

"Mr. Klick, whatever it is you are after, I cannot help.
I will tell you the same thing I told the police." He
smiled again, and now I understood. He thought *I* was
the police. "This office represents literally hundreds of
financial interests in the Bay Area. Pacific Rim retains
me as a signatory on their financial accounts handled by,
as you pointed out, the accounting firm of Mr. Michael
L. Tooley and Associates. It is simply a technicality to
insure no misuse of funds on the part of Mr. Tooley. Our
practice has no ties with Pacific Rim other than this."

"But who are your clients? I need to talk with your
clients."

"In my esteemed judgment, they don't need to talk
with you. I'm sorry, Mr. Klick."

"My clients are interested in buying the warehouse."

"Are you in commercial real estate? You strike me
more as the kind of man who delivers paper or chases
errant husbands who owe child payment," Hanright
said. "Skip tracers, we call them in my profession."

"I am not a PI, Mr. Hanright." I considered this. "Not
by profession, at least."

"Next time do your homework. The warehouse
couldn't be sold, even if my clients wanted to sell it. It's
been seized by the police, for reasons you will have to
find out on your own."

"I've got you worried," I observed.

"Don't flatter yourself."

"What is it that scares you? How easily I found you?"

"The door is the rectangle in the wall with the brass domed knob on it. I suggest you use it."

I stood, debating whether to push further, but Hanright had finished with me. "Before you get yourself in serious trouble, why don't you leave?" he said.

"The police?" I asked.

"Good-bye, Mr. Klick."

* * *

"Tooley was a washout," Alicia said from the other side of a heaping chef's salad. Her predominant color was pink today, except the teal sash around her waist.

"Hanright implied police involvement," I told her.

"Do tell."

"Nothing much to tell. If one were to continue this digging, I presume he—or she—would discover that both Hanright and Tooley were hired through yet another law firm, probably out of state. Hired in turn—"

"From another state."

"Exactly."

"And around and around it goes."

"At some point the chain leaves the country, to banks and firms on small islands."

"Like the Bahamas."

"My thoughts precisely."

"Which means we could spend months at this."

"Unlikely," I told her. "At some point, were we to pursue what federal types could not, I fear we would come across some bad luck."

"Of the unhealthy variety."

"Just a guess."

"I must admit," she said, "Tooley would appear to be on the up-and-up."

"I'm sure he is. Perhaps Hanright is too. He tells me the warehouse couldn't be sold, even if his clients wanted it to be. It's been impounded. It's a dead end, Alicia. It's over."

"It might come up for auction. That happens sometime."

"It might at that."

"Do we talk to the police?"

"We read the newspapers. We do some research. If the police are involved, it will have been in the press at some point. The police themselves won't answer questions concerning an active investigation. We spend the afternoon at the library, and then I'm taking you to dinner at Café Sport."

"That doesn't sound very romantic."

"Just wait until you see it. I think you'll change your mind."

* * *

Following dinner the red message light on my telephone was blinking. I called the desk. My partner, Bruce Warren, had phoned. A return call set up a lunch in Los Angeles for the following day.

Bruce had information about the warehouse, as well as a royalty job to discuss.

16

Moustache Café in Hollywood had a number of side-walk tables tucked under an awning. The menu explained that the patio was for smoking, the building nonsmoking. One of Bruce's bad habits is tobacco. He cuts down occasionally, but he's never quit for more than a month since the age of eight. His lungs are probably the color and consistency of freshly laid pavement.

He produced an Express Mail envelope, handing it to Alicia, who passed it to me. "From Craig Zaccardi," he said. "He's an aide to Montclaire, the congressman from Nebraska who heads the subcommittee on International Banking Ethics and Practices. It figures that Craig would be the first to reply."

"How's that?"

"My brother got him his job."

"That helps."

I ate a piece of dark bread, no butter. Before he had a chance to explain, I said, "Pacific Rim Leasing is under investigation by the feds for distributing gray-market electronics."

"You knew this already?" he asked.

"Yesterday, while I was out chasing down attorneys with zippered lips, Alicia found a few newspaper articles on the raid. Customs agents seized a quarter of a

million worth of stereos, faxes, copiers, and telephones.
None of the gear had been properly imported. No duty
had been paid."

"So that's why we can't find the owners," Bruce said.

"Exactly."

He looked at Alicia and me. "These fellows are in it
deep. Alpha Investments is in the file, naturally, which
means they're also under investigation, as is South Regional Development Corporation. It's jointly held by
Korean interests and something called Far East Development Corporation in Bangkok, which has a ten-per-
cent ownership."

"With all its banking handled offshore," Alicia said.

Bruce nodded. "Count on it."

"So how does that all translate?" I asked.

"Pacific Rim's assets are ridiculously small. Got to be a
dummy." He handed me the second page. "The warehouse is about all it owns." Alicia looked over my shoulder at the papers. "If someone ever finds their books,
ownership may or may not become more clear," Bruce
continued.

"Ownership of Pacific Rim, Alpha, or ownership of
the warehouse?" I asked.

"Same thing," Alicia answered. I was being distracted
by her breath on my neck. "This supports what you said,
Chris. Companies owning companies, which in turn
own a company that owns the warehouse. The chance
of ever tracing it back to what might be called 'real
people' is slight."

I accepted the next page from Bruce, a rundown of
Alpha Investments, one of the three companies controlling Pacific Rim. It was a photocopy of a piece of an
annual report. I was exceptionally aware that Alicia's
breathing stopped momentarily. I turned my head and
she sat back quickly. Her face was white as paste. I was
about to say something when she excused herself very
abruptly, rose from her chair, and left, threading her

way through the tables. I looked around the room at the other faces in the crowd. Something—or someone—had startled her. I noticed a group of four just being seated, but I didn't recognize any of them. Had she?

Bruce continued reading. "I don't know, Chris. I don't know what you're into here, but I'm reminded of an old Western, where the scout looks down from his horse and shakes his head. 'No more tracks' he says."

"That's your specialty." After all, Bruce made his living following paperwork.

"I *may* be able to follow the trail for you," he said to me, standing as Alicia returned. I followed suit. As we sat down I looked at her closely. Her eyes were hard. She was different. "And certainly," Bruce continued, "I can be more effective and less conspicuous than a government agency attempting the same kind of trace. But my point is, Chris, all it can possibly bring you is trouble. Do you actually think someone who went to all this trouble wants to be found? Do you think they will offer to sell you the property in question? No way, buddy. Flat out no way. And remember, if the owners are never found, the government will take the warehouse and eventually auction it, just as Alicia said."

"It doesn't matter," Alicia said. "It's a dead end. We stop here."

We both studied her, awaiting her explanation.

She shook her head. "It doesn't matter," she repeated.

"I'm not sure I understand," Bruce said.

"There is no further need to retain your services, Mr. Warren," she said very formally.

"I was just explaining to Chris that I can follow the trail, if that's what's you want. It is only that given the circum—"

"No. Thank you, no. That won't be necessary."

Our food arrived, and we began in silence. I had broiled sole with a tarragon sauce and a bottle of St.

Pauli Girl. Bruce had an expensive hamburger that came with only half a bun. Alicia stabbed at a spinach salad, eating precious little. Her mood hung over us heavily.

Partly to change the subject, Bruce began telling me about a man named Simon Monk. Monk had written advertising jingles for nearly fifteen years, and from everything Bruce had been able to turn up, he had been screwed out of every cent of his residuals. Bruce's end of things, the unraveling of exactly how the monies had been withheld and where they now could be found, would take a few more weeks, perhaps as long as two months, but the case promised an "absolutely staggering finder's fee," as he put it. Mr. Monk would become a very wealthy individual, if I could find him.

It was good to have these talks with Bruce. Not only did it remind me that I loved this business, but it gave me a finite edge to the time remaining in my "vacation." He was warning me that in a month or so I would be back on the road, and I appreciated the warning. We drank a toast to Mr. Monk. We held our glasses awaiting Alicia's participation. Bruce finally cleared his throat to draw her attention, his arm beginning to tremble.

"Oh!" she said, raising her wine cooler, which she had not touched.

"To Simon Monk," Bruce said.

"Who?" asked Alicia.

17

Alicia and I drove for a few minutes, and then I stopped the car and suggested we go for a walk. The few looks she cast in my direction revealed a woman puzzled and frightened.

I went around and opened the door for her, and she climbed out. I was beginning to think her mood was somehow a reaction to our intimacy, to something I had done.

"Something I said?" I asked. The sidewalk was clean, the houses on both sides of the small winding hill we climbed were from the era of old Hollywood, with red tile roofs and exotic landscaping.

"No, no," she said, surprise in her voice. She touched my arm lightly. "I'm sorry, Chris; just thinking, that's all."

"Some heavy thinking."

"Yes," she acknowledged.

"Anything you want to talk about?"

"No."

"I don't mean to pry, but why did you call off Bruce? That's the end of it, you know. Did you call your father when you left the table. Is that it?"

She tried to sound convincing, "My father! No, no. It's as Bruce said. The trail is too distant now. This is much

more complicated and involved than my father antici-
pated. Not worth the effort, I'm afraid. He'll just have to
find another warehouse."

"Was it someone at the restaurant?" I asked. "Did you
see someone you knew?"

She smiled privately. "No. You're sweet. I didn't see
anyone. It's just disappointing, isn't it?"

"It doesn't explain the sudden change in you."

She ignored the comment, pointing up the road instead.

Ahead of us a film crew filled one lane of the small
road. Cameras, gaffers, a director. Much confusion. We
walked past a Winnebago. In front of the motorized
monster, two stuntmen wearing blue jeans and white
long johns were having a series of wires taped to them.
We stopped to watch. The man doing the taping was
reviewing the upcoming scene with them. From what I
could gather, one of them was going to have a flare gun
shot into his stomach, whereupon he would catch fire
and then be gunned down by semiautomatic weapons
fire. Standard primetime fare. Watching them prepare
was fascinating. The wires, running from where the
bullets would "explode" beneath the stuntman's shirt,
were all connected to a wireless transmitter. A techni-
cian would detonate the various charges as the scene
demanded. The man taping the wires to the stuntman
became quiet as another man who had to be the director came over and also reviewed the scene. He was
concerned about the fire segment. All four of them reviewed the safety precautions. The man next to the one
being wired was responsible for wrapping the second
stuntman in fire blankets. As we stood there watching
only a short distance away, the second stuntman pulled
on a white hood that resembled a ski mask: the same
kind of fire-protective gear formula race car drivers don
before a race.

Something nagged at me. I had recently seen something similar and I couldn't place it.

"Five minutes!" someone yelled from over by the cameras.

The safety man responsible for helping them after the shot was holding his hood, slapping it against his leg. "Excuse me," I said to him, not knowing why.

He turned. "Yeah?"

"That's some sort of fireproof fabric, right?" I stepped forward and felt it.

He nodded. "That's the shit," he said.

When I touched it, I knew. This same fabric had been worn by Michael Morton, the pilot who had jumped to his death at the Butte Peak airport. I recalled the grisly sight of his broken body skewered by the metal stake, remembered thinking it odd he would wear an undershirt given the heat. "Same stuff as race car drivers wear?" I asked.

"That's right. We wear special clothing on top of this, mind you. But this is the shit. This saves your ass if things get outta hand."

Alicia and I watched for the next half hour as they staged the scene. When the cameras finally rolled, the stuntman's chest exploded in gunfire, and his legs burst into flames when another actor struck him with a lit flare. "Let's go back to the hotel," I said. "I have to make a phone call."

I felt fragile. I realized that I was still emotionally vulnerable, still unprepared for a woman's silence, her downcast eyes. The power of a woman troubled is a power to be reckoned with, and I had none of the necessary tools available to me—no humor, no pat remarks. I felt raw and exposed. She sprinkled salt generously into my wounds with her painful, selfish silence.

When we got out of the elevator on our floor I hesitated a moment, expecting the invitation that did not come. She just turned and walked away without me. I

caught my hip on the brushed aluminum ashtray that
protruded from the wall and grumbled a complaint, but
she didn't even glance in my direction, did not alter her
course in the least. The key went into the lock and she
disappeared.

* * *

I phoned the Screen Actors Guild and found that there
was a Michael Morton, which was the name of the dead
pilot, registered with them. I then reached Lyel by
phone. He sounded bad. Or sad. Drunk perhaps. I was
going to ask him what was troubling him, but I didn't. If
he didn't bring it up, then I wouldn't. He shut me out
with his silence. First Alicia, now Lyel. I seemed to draw
these repeating patterns constantly, like a blackjack
player drawing face cards; my bad moments did not
come in bursts or bits, but in discouraging streaks.

"I saw something this afternoon, long johns, and I
realized that our late pilot, Michael Morton, had indeed
intended to crash. He *expected* fire. He was prepared
for it. So I called the Screen Actors Guild, and found out
Morton's an active member. Called his agent—he
hadn't worked in months. He told his agent he was
going to Idaho for show work, meaning an air show. His
agent only handles the film end of things. I have a hunch
the Butte Peak airport was Morton's gig. He *intended* to
crash, Lyel. Do you understand what that implies?"

"Sometimes it overwhelms the senses, and like it or
not we are buried in our own reluctance to understand.
We all—I think all of us are capable of understanding,
but how often do we try? Really try? Seldom. We seldom
try."

He was most certainly drunk. Off on a Lyelism. If
allowed, he might ramble on for hours. I cut him off.
"The pilot," I reminded him. "The crash *was* intentional."

"They killed Candy, Klick."

His tone of voice sent shivers through me.

I was suddenly back in her house with her, asking her to let *me* do the snooping around City Hall.

"Dan Norton's calling it an accidental overdose. 'Suicide.' Bullshit. Her killers are amateurs, Christopher. They don't even know their drugs. Who goes out on bennies lying down? Christ, the girl would have been doing a hundred thousand RPMs in neutral, with all the speed she had in her. They probably mashed them up and made her drink them in something. Then they would have had to wait. Probably thought she would nod out. Amateurs. I wonder what they thought when she suddenly became Superwoman. Must have taken some effort to hold her down. Waited until her heart popped like an overinflated bike tire. I saw the body. Bruises on both wrists. There are a thousand and one ways to kill a person, right? I mean there are plenty of ways to do it so the person doesn't suffer. Cranking a person up on speed is not one of them."

"I'm coming home," I said into the phone, uncertain he was even listening.

18

Alicia clung to her silence for the return flight to Butte Peak, further isolating me. We both had two drinks. Mine made me think; hers put her to sleep. The steward continually bumped my right shoulder as he passed.

We had a layover in San Francisco, another in Boise. Finally the Horizon Air Dash 8 approached Butte Peak from the north, and I was reminded of the recent political turmoil over the growth of the airport. And of the crash. I gazed out the window at the twinkling lights below. My sorrow weighed a thousand pounds: I was surprised the plane had made it off the ground.

* * *

Lyel was fast asleep on the couch. Derby wagged her entire body at me when I entered the living room. She whined and nuzzled me. A half empty bottle of Meyer's stood by an empty glass. Lyel wouldn't be moving for another day or two.

I didn't head to Candy's, I headed to her sister's. I knew now what to look for.

Except for porch lights, all the condominiums were dark. Thanks to Candy, I already knew the key was tucked in behind the first 2 of the 212 tacked to a slab of the aluminum siding.

Once inside, I switched on the light and started looking around. The kitchen, a small dining table, and a sitting area—a couch, coffee table, and two chairs—all shared one large space, divided only by a kitchen counter. I tried the kitchen first, checking all the drawers. Nothing. The bedroom next. Drawers, closet shelf, under the mattress, nightstand, behind the mirror: nothing unusual. I tried the adjoining bathroom and was disappointed. It seemed to me that Bert would have kept what I was after, and I couldn't imagine that she would have had enough forethought to place it in a safe-deposit box.

I tried all the likely places; I found nothing.

Searching a place is something I've done many, many times; often it's how I begin trying to find a person. My usual technique involves a thorough but quick surface search followed by a second phase of deeper penetration, and a third of complete and utter meticulousness.

I disassembled two of the framed posters that hung on the bedroom walls, one of an actor, the other of a male athlete with a washboard stomach, hoping to find something between poster and backing. Nothing. The two in the living room, a Renoir and a Warhol, defeated me as well. I checked beneath the loose shelf paper in all the kitchen drawers and cabinets.

I finally found what I was looking for sealed inside a Ziploc freezer bag in the gray plastic drip tray that fit below the refrigerator. It was a good spot—easily accessible, not easily or accidentally discovered. I sat down on one of the kitchen stools and spread the contents out on the imitation oak veneer of the counter.

There were four envelopes in all. I hadn't expected that many. It meant the blackmail had been going on longer than I had imagined.

Two were empty. Why keep them? Souvenirs? The third contained three crisp one-hundred-dollar bills. My heart sank; my throat tightened. From everything I had learned about her, Bert McGreggor was not the type to leave three hundred in cash behind. Bert McGreggor was not only missing—she was dead.

The fourth envelope had been left specifically for someone like me; she had left it for me before she even knew I existed. It contained a single piece of paper. At the top was a legal description of property boundaries written in a delicate hand, presumably hers: *Township 2 South, range 18, section 10, excluding the highway.* Below this were four dates spanning the last year, each about three months apart. Alongside each date were names with which I had become familiar in the last few days: Alpha Investments, South Regional Development Corporation, Alderman Associates. I read them twice. These same companies had holdings in Pacific Rim Leasing, the company under investigation that owned the warehouse south of Redwood City. At the bottom of the page were two names: Brandon Cousin and Jim Corwin. Cousin I knew. Corwin I had never heard of.

At that instant the front door crashed open. I jumped. "Police!" said the voice of the unseen man. "Freeze!" Even cops watch too much TV.

My reaction was immediate. The envelopes went inside the plastic bag and I winged the bag against the near wall; it slipped behind the couch. It was as smooth as a Magic Johnson three-point attempt.

"In here," I called out.

"Hands on the counter," the patrolman said, crouching as he rounded the corner, the black circular eye of his .38 staring me down. His partner appeared at the back door. I obeyed. I don't like looking down gun barrels.

"I'm an investigator. I'm on a case," I told him. "Chris Klick. Dan Norton will back me up."

"Dan Norton sent me over here, buddy. You're under arrest."

19

I had to let it ring for well over a minute. Lyel finally answered in a voice that didn't seem to belong to him. I explained my predicament. "You're saying you want me to bail you out," he said.

I acknowledged that I did.

"I'll have to shower and change. Cold shower, I'm afraid." He asked if I had called his attorney. I had not. He complained about what a pain in the ass I was, sounding much more sober. Then he told me he would take care of everything—in the morning—and hung up. I attempted a protest, but that annoying noise of Ma Bell's grated in my ear.

Police Chief Dan Norton and I knew each other well enough to say hello in the market. He turned out to be a rules-for-the-sake-of-rules man. I asked him what was going on. He pointed out I was busted on a B and E. I explained that I was working for Candy McGreggor. He reminded me that I was not a registered private investigator, and even if I was, it was still a B and E. We talked about Candy's death. He bristled at my suggestion that someone had assisted her in the consumption of pills. He said that I'd been talking to Lyel, and I told him he was right.

"Your deputy told me you were the one who called in

the B and E, Dan. What the hell are you doing on dispatch at two in the morning?"

"I wasn't on dispatch."

"So you were tipped off," I said. We both knew it. "Doesn't that ring a little funny?" I asked.

"You broke the law, Klick. It just so happens your headlights and that noisy truck of yours woke up a neighbor and I got a call. Besides, how things ring is not my concern in this town."

"You're feeling the pressure. Is that it?"

"No, no," he replied sarcastically. "This town is real used to disappearances and drug overdoses."

"And plane accidents."

He winced.

"Careful, Klick. You're on dangerous ground."

"Who ordered the highway closed for repair on the day of the plane crash? Was it Cousin?" He didn't have to answer. His look told me it had been.

"I can help, you know?" I said.

"I doubt it."

"I can put my nose where it doesn't belong."

"So I've noticed."

"Candy wasn't a suicide. She was murdered. And Bert McGreggor didn't just take off. She was killed also. If she had left town she would have taken her cash with her, and she didn't. She left it hidden at home. I just found it, along with the legal description of a piece of property. Bert McGreggor was blackmailing someone. And the someone paid, which meant she knew what she was talking about. My guess is it involves the relocation of the airport—and that involves Cousin."

Norton looked stunned. Some of this obviously made sense to him. "How much of this can you prove?"

"Right now?"

"Yes, right now."

"None."

He shook his head. "Then I'd watch who I repeated it to, and I'd keep a shotgun in the rack of that pickup."

"We may need some help on this," I said.

"I'm here, Klick. I'll do what I can."

20

Lyel occupied his couch awkwardly, propped up on one elbow, his unshaven chin in his hand. His attorney, Terry Hogue, had finally bailed me out at one in the morning. Lyel's opinion of me had suffered; I was the child who had done wrong: I had not checked in with him before leaving, and now Candy McGreggor was dead.

"Bert had money hidden beneath the refrigerator."

"Blackmail?"

"Blackmail," I confirmed.

"Bottom line?" he asked. He positioned an over-stuffed pillow beneath his ribs. Lyel has a big, bony head with a protruding brow and brown hair that hangs lifelessly from his scalp; with his head at this angle, it hung down like seaweed.

"Norton's feeling the pressure. The mayor is his boss, after all. Cousin's name was on Bert's piece of paper."

"Why?" He came up off the pillow and looked at me inquisitively, the spark lit.

"You won't like it."

"Cousin is manager of the airport," he began.

"Bravo. And what's the most controversial political topic of the year?"

"I'll give you that much. I admit that much," he said.

"What topic had all but gone away until that crash?"

He nodded. "After the night landings began," I went on, "a citizen's committee was formed. Protest died down. A couple months later you couldn't find mention of the airport in either of the papers." Lyel gave me another nod. "No more talk of moving the airport. If there was talk, it was only in that committee." I gave him a second to think about it. "Since the crash, that same citizens group is calling for the airport to be moved. Irate parents are standing up at town council meetings, talking of their children waking up screaming from the noise of the landings."

"They never should have permitted night landings. Not over the town. That was their mistake," Lyel said.

"They've made many mistakes, including the night landings. And who has steadfastly defended the decisions of the airport commission?"

"Brandon Cousin."

"Exactly."

His brow furrowed tightly into a knot of leathery creases. "As manager, it's his job to keep the peace, to keep the townspeople happy."

"And he has failed at that job. So the question arises, was his failure determined by a change in public opinion, as it would appear, or did he perhaps *intend* to fail?"

"I'll be damned, Klick," Lyel said, his face animated, his voice tight. "Cousin—and who else? he couldn't be acting alone—staged the crash to get the public back into it. He's found a way to profit by moving the airport. He cries like he doesn't want it moved, but he actually *does*."

"Bingo! Cousin has to be involved. It's just a little too much that the highway was detoured the very day of the crash."

"You're saying Cousin kept the highway clear to reduce the chance a passing car would be hit when the plane crashed; he bought himself some insurance."

"Yes, as mayor he would know the highway repair schedule."

"But can we prove all this?" Lyel asked.

"That's just what Norton said."

"Can we?" He scratched his head. "It depends how careful they were. And we need to know *who* they were. You can bet they would need some people in their pocket. The county assessor, for one."

"Jim Corwin," I said.

"Who's that?" he asked.

"Just a guess. I have a feeling he's our star witness."

* * *

Within seconds of parking the truck in my own driveway, I saw the flicker of headlights off to my right that meant visitors. When those headlights went dark, still nearly a half-mile from my house, and I continued to hear the engine, I grew concerned.

I kept a loaded Smith and Wesson hidden under the front seat of the truck. Originally I had carried it to finish off so-called road-kills: there was no more disheartening sight than a fatally wounded deer or antelope hit by your truck, forced to suffer because you had no weapon. The term road-kill was a misconception; in my experience the animal usually lived, sometimes for hours, writhing in pain. The Smith and Wesson was there to deal with this dilemma, even though shooting a deer out of season, even a wounded road-kill, was considered illegal and carried a stiff fine.

I had used the Smith and Wesson several times.

The vehicle stopped out there in the dark and I heard the conscientious quiet click of the doors shutting. Doors—*two* of them.

This was not good. I didn't have the time, or the

inclination, to make a break for the house. I pulled into the shadow, Smith and Wesson in hand.

The footfalls on the gravel came straight down the lane. Two of them came through the gate and entered my drive. A big one and a skinny one: Slim and his buddy. At this point it was official: they were trespassing. That still carried some legal weight in the West. I heard them whisper to each other, though I couldn't make out the words. I dropped lower to use the starry glow of the night sky, the powerful ribbon of the Milky Way, as a backdrop, picking up the two in silhouette. I recognized one of them immediately by his slight frame: Slim. They crept stealthily up to the cabin, moved to a window and tried to see inside. I had to make a quick decision: wait until they split up and try to work on them one by one, or go after them now before they split. The decision was made for me: they divided immediately. Slim disappeared around the far side of the house. The bigger one stayed put, just across the gravel drive from me, his shoulder pushed up against a tall blue spruce at the corner of the cabin. I didn't see any weapons, though I knew this one's knife well enough. I didn't intend to be introduced to it again.

I drew the Smith and Wesson to the low-ready position—aimed at the ground but ready in a single motion to be directed at whatever target presented itself—and slipped to my left, trying as best I could to be directly behind the bigger, bearded, hard-featured man, who in silhouette reminded me of a logger. I was not as quiet as I had hoped to be and the Logger turned around in a state of surprise. I was still fifteen feet away from him. At fifteen feet the Smith and Wesson and I were a good team. Anything much over that and it's difficult to deliver an effective bullet pattern. As he reached for his back pocket, I maintained my position of low-ready and hissed, "Lose it!" A knife, sticking half out of his back, from his pocket. "On the ground. Arms out," I ordered.

The man hit the gravel swiftly. I moved sideways toward him, the gun aimed carefully away from both of us. "You're trespassing," I said to him.

"Fuck off," he said.

"Reach back and ease the knife out. As it comes out of your pocket, drop it immediately." My heart was pumping a little too strongly. I pulled my finger off the trigger. The knife tumbled out onto the gravel. I kicked it away. "Be still."

We waited for Slim. I had my hands full. With my heart at a gallop and the adrenaline pumping, it was everything I could do to maintain this divided attention between both corners of the house and the Logger, his face in the gravel.

Slim finally rounded the corner to my left, by the garage. I couldn't see him well in the darkness, and he apparently couldn't see me at all—or perhaps he mistook me for the Logger, but I knew this house. He did not.

As he took another two steps forward, the motion-sensing flood lights on the outside of the garage came on in a blinding display of several hundred watts. These spots had been intended to prevent the local skunk from raiding my trash, but they now served to distract and simultaneously blind Slim.

In a way, they blinded *me* as well—not visually, because I expected them, but their effect on Slim stole my attention, and the Logger was much faster than I thought. He leaped to his feet, kidney-punched me, knocked the gun loose, and then kicked my legs out from beneath me. As we came up together, his knife was held, blade first, at the bridge of my nose. He pulled his way behind me, keeping the knife there.

Slim moved in with his pea-shooter, but kept his distance and effected an angle to leave his buddy out of his line of fire.

"You've been practicing," I said. "No fair." I won-

dered if he could see the hairs on the nape of my neck
stand at attention.

The one behind me tugged painfully on my earlobe.
Slim said, "We warned you about this, Klick."

The Logger felt obliged to add, "Musicians like their
ears, don't they?"

"Affirmative," I told him, still hoping for a better look
at his face. As it was my second encounter, both in the
dark but now with light shining, I wanted to stamp that
image indelibly into my mind. I glanced over my shoulder at him. He lacked a chin, which explained the
beard. He used the knife to direct my attention back to
Slim.

Slim said, "When I was a kid I used to place a rubber
band on my wrist so I wouldn't forget something. Eventually that rubber band became irritating enough to
remind me. We want to make sure you don't forget that
you're a pain in the ass, Klick. You keep sticking your
nose where it don't belong, and next time we'll take
your nose." He nodded. The Logger slit the lobe of my
ear where it joined to my neck. It was such a sharp knife
that briefly it was painless. But as my blood spilled down
onto my shirt, the pain stung into me.

"To hell with your nose," the one said from behind.
"We'll take one of your *cojones* next time. And that's
usually the end of you." He stepped away from me.

Head wounds, neck wounds, tend to bleed a lot. My
ear proved no exception. I was feeling lightheaded.

Slim looked slightly psychotic. He was *enjoying* this, I
realized. He wanted to stand there and watch me bleed.
"Then we won't be seeing you around again, will we,
Klick?"

"That would be rather foolish of me, wouldn't it?"

Logger stepped up and toyed with my cut ear.
"That's not an answer."

"What can I say?"

He jerked hard on my earlobe, and my stomach

turned. I thought for a moment that he might simply tear it off. "You can say that we won't be hearing from you again. Or, like I just said, we can cut off one of your oysters and watch you eat it."

I had read somewhere that professional wrestlers in Japan can suck their testicles up into their bodies before battle. It was a skill I thought I might want to learn soon. "I am, as of this moment, back on vacation," I stated definitely.

"Now *that's* music to *my* ears," Slim said, nodding. He watched too much television.

"Don't fuck this up, Klick. A guy as big as you would sound a little queer talking in falsetto . . . if you lived that long."

Logger used the knife persuasively to help lead me first to my knees and then facedown. Slim said, "Five minutes like that or it's lesson number two."

I heard their footsteps on the gravel as they walked away.

If I had had a gun in hand, I would have shot them both in the back.

Fair's fair.

21

Lyel came to my rescue and saw to my stitches at the emergency room. He consoled me back at his place with a few deep Glenlivets and his philosophy on how to deal with such people, which tended toward the extreme: he was leaning toward torture by the time I declined the third drink. Scotch on top of painkillers was a little like taking an unprotected right from Tyson.

Bruce phoned at nine-thirty my time the next morning, eight-thirty L.A. time. I am able to read Bruce like a book; I can tell what kind of mood he's in and whether he has good news or bad just from the way he says hello. Today he had good news, interesting news of some sort. I knew it the moment he asked me, "Have you had your coffee yet?"

"Been up for hours," I told him.

"Those board members? Not a living soul among them," he said. "All nonpeople. It's a complete front. We're not talking offshore, we're talking off-planet here."

"Nonpeople?"

"I misspoke. Not exactly nonpeople. The corporation was set up in the early seventies before the feds were hip to the death registry scam. The same way you arranged your fake identities: make fake people out of dead people. Those formerly dead people can get social security numbers, be paid salaries, serve on boards, even pay taxes."

"You're saying the boards of these companies are made up of dead people?" I asked.

"You don't need living people. At least, not many—someone has to run things, after all. What you need are minutes of board meetings, a phone number, and a mailing address. For an office, you establish a mail drop, a phone drop—one of those blind call-forwarding services. It wouldn't take much. No one could trace it back to you."

"And there's no way at all to trace these nonpeople? I mean, it's really that effective?"

"Depends on how casual they are and how many they are. With a board of trustees of nonpeople, there is actually no way of telling how many *living* people are behind the front. The mail drops, the phone services, the bank accounts, the accountants and attorneys, that's where you'll find them, if you'll find them at all: through the services they use. Even crooked corporations need servicing. Lyel's National Credit Bureau friend may be able to help you there. A full credit run might give you one of the mail drops, or even a legit address."

He agreed to keep digging. I told him we'd do the same.

* * *

Lyel and I were sitting around the kitchen table. He was making notes; I was studying my most recent art loan.

Alongside Blue Hair, an oil pastel by Julie Scott, now hung his girlfriend, the subject of another Scott painting, *Mud Lake, Still Bottom.* It depicts a hard-featured woman standing naked in water up to her neck. I had renamed the painting *Molina,* and for the first time I saw in her a resemblance, however vague, to Alicia.

Something about the confidence in her. *Molina* was only on loan until Julie sold her; I couldn't afford three thousand dollars for a painting. Ever confident that I would trace the ownership of the warehouse, despite the present setbacks, I considered using the finder's fee to acquire *Molina*. Blue Hair had grown as fond of her as I had, I was sure of that, and he deserved to have someone up there keeping him company. Especially a woman with no clothes on.

Seeing *Molina* and thinking of Alicia, I recalled her sudden change during lunch in L.A.

"Something's just occurred to me," I said.

"I'm listening," said Lyel. He headed straight to the refrigerator, checked my rations, and helped himself to a bowl of spoon-size shredded wheat, which he brought to the table. His cheeks undulated while I explained.

"In L.A., at lunch a weird thing happened when Alicia looked over my shoulder at this list—at the board of trustees for Alpha Investments. At the time I thought maybe she had seen someone in the restaurant. She excused herself and came back with red eyes; like she'd been crying. I didn't connect it to the list until just now—"

"Guided by your prick again, it sounds like to me." This he said with a mouthful of cereal.

I glared.

Lyel reciprocated.

I gave in. "Probably."

"The list," he said, reminding me.

"Yes. Now I'm thinking it was the list. Dead people every one of them, Bruce tells me."

"Precautions," he said, bubbling milk onto the table.

"That's how he sees it."

"But you think Alicia recognized a name."

"I'm sure of it. Alicia Gebhardt knew one of those names. That confuses me."

"Women always confuse you," Lyel said.

22

I rang the Gebhardts' doorbell and a few moments later was greeted by a young woman wearing a Speedy Bee T-shirt. Speedy Bee is a Snow Lake housecleaning outfit.

Before I spoke a word she said, "Mr. Gebhardt is out."

I told her I was there to see Alicia.

"Well right at the moment," she said in a squeaky voice, "you'd see a little too much. She's out back stretched out on a chaise soaking up rays. Not exactly part of my job description, but why don't I give her a shout. Give me a sec."

"No problem. I could use a minute on the phone anyway." I pointed to Gebhardt's study.

"Sure thing." She made it fifteen feet across the room with the quicksand carpet before turning and asking, "You are?"

"Chris Klick."

"That's easy enough." She hurried on.

I headed directly to Gebhardt's walnut desk and conducted a thorough surface canvassing. A two-line Panasonic telephone with auto-dial buttons. It showed good taste: I have the same kind. A Rolodex, which I flipped through quickly, trying to log a few names, but there weren't many in it, most of the paper tiles blank.

A monstrous stack of bills to the right, secured by a glass paperweight. Desk calendar open to yesterday. I glanced up at the open door. The Speedy Bee had yet to return. I flipped back several days. Two were blank. One had a name with a question mark beside it: *Stoney?* I continued to flip back through the calendar. There was my name and number. Underlined, twice. I turned back to the page it'd been open to. Guessing I still had a minute. I looked at the labels next to the phone's autodial buttons. The first read 911, the second ALICIA, the third through seventh had names I didn't recognize. The rest were blank. It was the blank slots that interested me. I was counting on Gebhardt being as lazy and/or cautious as I am. For those of us who are lazy, a recently added number doesn't merit the effort of bothering to fill out the little label. I often wait until I fill up two or three blank slots, finding them easy enough to memorize, before going to the trouble of writing the names in. Sometimes one might not want to advertise: my mother's home number is on my Panasonic's autodial, but I didn't write MOM on my phone.

I pushed the first button. The line rang four times, at which point a woman's taperecorded voice answered with the number, five two five six, and a message inviting me to speak. I hung up and tried the next: a single beep, indicating no number had been input. Six more down the line, all unused. I hit the last button. The dialer beeped out a number.

It rang.

I waited.

A man's voice answered, western and dry, like Roy Rogers with laryngitis. "Brandon Cousin . . . Hello?"

I hung up just as the woman poked her head into the room.

"Alicia says come on back," she said, not the slightest bit of concern on her face.

The mayor of Butte Peak—the manager of the airport

—occupied an unmarked station on Gebhardt's phone. Why?

* * *

Alicia was stretched out on a large beach towel draped over a mauve chaise alongside the pool pavillion, her flawless youthful skin bronzed deeply. Her suit reminded me of mylar. There wasn't much of it. The sun caught the fine blond hairs on her smooth belly. Her fingernails and toenails were painted the faint orange-red cast of ripe persimmon fruit, a color echoed by her lipstick. The lipstick appeared fresh. She reacted to my hello with sun-drenched slowness. I bent over to greet her, feeling some of the lipstick remain on my cheek.

"You want to join me?" she asked in the indolent voice of a person just awakened.

I thought about our stay at the St. Francis.

"I like joining with you very much," I said, eliciting a squinting sun-strained glance from beneath her delicate eyelids.

She failed to say anything. "It's about these names," I offered. Her lips puckered. "The board of trustees for Alpha Investments," I added, as if I had to explain.

"What about them?" she asked, maintaining her vocal edge of indifference.

"When we were in L.A. with Bruce—"

"I already explained that. How many times must a girl apologize?" Another quick glance, just to drive home her point.

"I don't think I buy it. The explanation, I mean. You recognized one of the names, didn't you?" How could two people who had wrapped limb around limb, who had physically shared a most intimate and wondrous moment, conduct a discussion like total strangers, even adversaries? It was moments such as these that scared me away from relationships.

"One of the names? What are you talking about, Chris?"

"Alpha Investments. We're talking about Alpha Investments. We're talking about a company whose board of directors doesn't exist."

"Did my father pay you yet? He'll pay you a substantial kill fee."

"I'm not sure I like that term. You're avoiding answering me. Why?"

"Chris, I'm not avoiding anything."

"A girl was killed while we were gone. Did you know that?"

Her brow knitted, and she finally took the trouble to sit up and look fully at me. In the bright sunlight, her eyes took on a deep luminescence. "What is that supposed to mean?"

"Your father suggested you hire me, didn't he?"

"We've covered that."

"I'm not so sure we've covered it. I have a feeling it was more of a fly-by. How well does your father know Brandon Cousin?"

"Who?"

"The mayor of Butte Peak. The manager of the Butte Peak–Snow Lake airport. Brandon Cousin," I repeated. The sun was hot. I felt a drop of perspiration run down my sternum.

"I don't know him."

"But what about your father?" The thing about women like Alicia Gebhardt: they're born actresses. I had seen her perform.

"I don't keep track of his friendships."

"Why the cold shoulder?" I asked, not realizing I had said it until too late.

She reached out a searching hand like a blind person, but the gesture was oddly patronizing.

"Your attitude changed after you read the names of the Alpha board," I insisted.

"Don't be silly."

"Silly?" I waited. She peered at me again, shielding her eyes with her hand. "A woman was *killed*, Alicia," I said. "Two women—and your father's involved."

"Get out of here, Chris. Now!" she snapped, suddenly furious.

"I need your help, Alicia. The names—"

"Now!"

I turned to leave, the sweet pungent smell of Hawaiian Tropic following me through the doorway. I heard her stand up, but I wasn't about to turn around, to look back. I didn't want to see her face.

I had been suckered by that face. By that body. I wasn't about to let it happen again.

23

I returned to Roberta McGreggor's condominium that evening, a risk I would have rather not taken, but I saw no way around it. This time I had my Detonics in a holster at my side, hidden inside the dark windbreaker I wore.

If I involved Dan Norton at this stage and he proved too pressured by those above him, the evidence I had tossed behind the couch might end up locked away in a police file. My best bet was to retrieve the envelopes and then turn them over to Dan myself. At least that way I had the information I was after: the legal description of the mystery property. But I had a problem: last time, someone had seen me enter the condo and had tipped the police.

No one had followed me then, nor was anyone following me this time—I had made certain of that. But there was no telling if the place was being watched. The joy of living in a small town is also a problem for a man in my profession: everyone watches out after everyone else's business, and everyone does everyone else favors. There was only the one door, and I went through it. If someone was watching, I had just been seen. I kept that in mind. I knew what I was after; I could be in and out in a matter of seconds.

I went directly to the living room with its rental show-room furniture and pulled the couch away from the wall. The plastic-clad package was right where I had tossed it. I had briefly worried that if on my first visit the place had been under surveillance, perhaps someone had gone in after me and searched the apartment as I had—and had discovered what I had. But evidently not.

I hid the bag under my windbreaker and left the apartment as quickly as I had arrived, debating with myself briefly before wiping off the key and returning it to its hiding place. I didn't want it to be found in my possession. I climbed into my truck, headed back to the north entrance to Broadmore Road, and made the peaceful drive back to Lyel's guesthouse. Derby was awaiting me on the front porch, tail going like a metro-nome.

*   *   *

Identifying the parcel of land indicated in Roberta Mc-Greggor's hidden notes amounted to a quick stop at the county courthouse the next day and a visit with her friend Rita, who showed me on a county map where the sector was located: south of the valley's only flashing light, in the direction of Twin Falls, on the other side of Timmerman Hill.

As my tilted truck crested Timmerman Hill at forty miles an hour I looked off into the arid, seemingly end-less expanse of sage-covered open range, beyond which I could make out a formation like a black carpet, the northernmost edge of the ten-thousand-year-old lava flow. This coal-colored amoebic landscape met the azure sky far, far in the distance, where white clouds hung suspended from a scorching sun. As if to confirm my suspicions, a spark of blinding silver light stung my eyes, a reflection from a commercial aircraft passing thirty thousand feet overhead.

I turned right onto a county road of dirt and crushed granite and passed through a break in a seemingly endless fence. It was very flat here, grand and expansive, a high-desert plateau, the upper gray-green tips of the craggy sage bushes bending and waving before the efforts of a determined southerly wind. There are millions of acres like this in the West, land where a few score cattle forage for summer food, inhabited by snowshoe rabbits and elk in the winter months. Dry, parched, dusty land, occasionally transformed by wildfire, made more grassy, but for the most part barren, financially impractical land that served more as a welcome mat to the high mountain forests of evergreen. It looked no different than other ranges, the prairie bulging and rippling toward the impending foothills in wavelike contours. And yet as I continued through the parcel and eventually crossed another fence line, I was able to picture a pattern of half-mile ribbons of black asphalt, perfectly straight lanes of blue landing lights, and the customary red and white outbuildings and radar installations that rim any airport. I could see gigantic white numbers painted on the tarmac, and a checkered wind sock. I could see Hertz and Avis, long-term and short-term parking, buses and air charter groups, bars, restaurants, and even an inexpensive motel or two. I could see money falling from the deep blue sky and blanketing this virtual wasteland.

I could see the black scar of an explosion from here.

I approached the charred area on foot. I was about a mile away from the state highway, which, because of the contours of the land, I could no longer see. Stubborn field grass had already begun to obscure the evidence of the explosion, and once I was immediately on top of it, it vanished completely, looking like a section of lava flow. It was only visible from a distance. But it was quite obviously recent, and my heart began to pound strongly as I noticed a tiny piece of red plastic that I recognized as part of a taillight. I bent over and picked it up; sunlight sparkled from it beautifully. Pocketing it, I began my search.

* * *

Nick, grease-smeared to his elbows, was working on the differential of a '72 four-by-four pickup. I dumped my armful of car parts on the cement floor by the door. The noise caught his attention. "You again?" he asked rhetorically.

I nodded.

"You won't be driving it," he said, looking at the small pile of parts.

"No."

He detected my concern; he must have, for he put the box wrench down and ducked out from beneath the chassis. He didn't say anything more for a minute. One by one he studied the various parts. He examined them closely, dipping one in cleaning solution and rubbing the black off it.

"I brought any pieces I could find with numbers on them."

He nodded slowly, eyes fixed on the part in his hand. I saw him swallow hard. His eyes glassed up.

"Who did this?" he asked. There was anger and grief in his voice.

"That's what I'm trying to find out," I said.

"They had to do it for a reason. Right?" I didn't say anything. "Makes it a lot worse that I've been so fucking mad at her."

"Are they from her Mustang?"

"You bet. This piece here . . . this was part of a custom transmission. Put it in myself. Gotta be her rig."

"Two guys," I said, "I need to know their names. Maybe work security at the airport, maybe not. One's real skinny and oily. His buddy is built like a brick shithouse. They're kids. Early twenties, tops. Sound familiar?"

"No." I believed him. But I was worried that I had told him too much.

"This is nothing to mess with, Nick."

"I can see that," he said, turning the part slowly in his hands.

24

Lyel wanted to see the property, so he drove us in his Wagoneer to the crest of Timmerman Hill and then slowed to a stop. He shifted into four-wheel-drive low, pulled off the pavement, and followed a deeply rutted off-road trail to the summit, from which we had a breathtaking view both north and south.

He pushed the buttons on the driver's control panel, lowering both power windows simultaneously.

"It's down there," I said, pointing out the tract of land.

"Flat. Wide. Perfect for an airport. I forgot to tell you, what with Candice's death and all, that while you were gone, Gebhardt attended a public meeting of the airport commission. Cousin was there as well, of course, and if I had to guess—with the benefit of hindsight—I would say that since the subject of the meeting was the selection of land parcels for airport relocation, and since you were caught snooping around the airport, he had another reason to want you out of the way for a few days. Gebhardt and Cousin didn't sit together; they didn't even talk. But if a picture is worth a thousand words, so are facial expressions. The way those two eyed each other at several different times during the meeting was enough to convince me they shared something."

The gentle wind blew through the car. It felt wonderful. A red-tailed hawk soared effortlessly above a distant bluff, searching the plateau below for a meal.

"Could the two of them do it alone?"

"The *three* of them; up until a few weeks ago, James Corwin was the county real estate assessor. With his help and silence, Gebhardt could sell and resell that land down there back and forth between his dummy companies three or four times, each time escalating the land's value. He'd be selling to himself, so he'd never lose any money. When time comes, the county may acquire the airport land by use of eminent domain, but the price they pay will be the assessed value. And that is most often determined by the last price paid for it. They will then put construction contracts out to bid on building the airport. Lowest bid will probably get it, but Cousin will know the lowest bid. He can rig the contracts if he has a partner."

"Like Alpha Investments."

"One Anthony Gebhardt."

"You're keeping something from me," I said.

"Anthony Gebhardt, for all his flash and pretense, is pyramided to within an inch of his life. He's busted. Flat broke busted."

I recalled the stack of bills on the man's desk. "The house?"

"Rented. Three months back rent owed."

"How'd you find this out?"

"A half hour before you showed up I got a fax from Cory Richbiel, a friend of mine at a credit bureau. Called around about the property. Cory told me about the back rent. He's out about six grand so far. He's pissed."

"So it's Gebhardt behind Pacific Rim and Alpha and the others?"

"Alicia may be able to answer that, from what you said, but it makes sense, doesn't it?"

"Not really. Why the hell hire me?"

"He hired you to find out if you could find him. He knew the way the feds work: they take their time. You promised to be much faster. He would know how tightly he had spun his web. If you could trace that warehouse back to him, then he had big trouble, because that meant the feds eventually could—and would. But he obviously didn't believe you'd be able to. He was willing to pay big money to find out if he was right. His screw-up was sending his daughter along. From what you've said, she recognized a name on your list of nonpeople. You need to explore that further. We need a confirmation from her to know how accurate our theory is."

"Cousin tipped him off," I said. "Cousin knew which way the wind would blow concerning the airport, and from what you just said, we have to assume that although the commission is going to look at several parcels, the one they're going to choose will be Alpha's. Is this the only parcel on this side of Timmerman?"

"Of the ones put forward at the meeting, yes. But how the hell did you know that, Klick?"

"Weather. The FAA has a big say in this, don't forget, and the other side of Timmerman is just too foggy most of the winter. This side is clear. They all may be flat, they all may be big, but if this one has the better weather it will get the nod. But I'm still not real clear on how they bump up the price of the parcel so much. How much are we talking about, anyway?"

"If they had enough lead time to make three or four sales, allowing a few months between each sale, they could probably triple the value. Alpha buys two thousand acres at a thousand an acre and resells a few months later for fifteen hundred to one of Gebhardt's other dummy companies, two grand an acre a few months later, and so on. Churn it up to about three thousand an acre. Higher than any other land around, but given the increase in property values up valley, not enough to send up any red flags. When the county finally claims it and pays out, the profit would be four million dollars on an initial investment of, say, five hundred thousand. And the way this thing was structured, he borrowed the five against the electronics business. If your information is correct, then he avoided duty on the electronics he had warehoused. Probably paid twenty-five cents on the dollar for what he could sell the stuff for over here. The feds busted the electronics business by busting his warehouse, and suddenly not only was he out that investment, but the land loan looked sour. He needs cash. A lot of cash."

"He needs the airport land to be sold *immediately,*" I said.

"Yes. And at a substantial profit."

"So he and Cousin invent a crash to raise the public outcry and light a fire under the airport commission," I suggested. "Get things moving. Ramrod it through."

"Why not?" asked Lyel. "They didn't intend for the pilot to be killed. He was an expert. He was supposed to survive and tell a good story. He's a professional actor, after all."

"But along comes Roberta McGreggor and spoils all their plans," I said. "She notices the turnover of that parcel down there." I pointed. "Too much activity. Corwin's name, no doubt, is on every piece of paper. She squeezes him to raise capital to pay off her debts. Corwin or Cousin or Gebhardt—or all of them—play along for a while. I found several envelopes at her place. But eventually one or all have a change of heart. Too many fingers in the pie."

We were silent then, both of us staring down at the site of the future airport. "Murder for love is irrational, but somehow understandable," I said. "Murder for profit . . . that one really sticks in my craw."

"I hear you."

"So they must be revealed. And their plot must never come to fruition."

"It won't be easy," Lyel warned. He stared out at the horizon.

"But can it be done?"

He finished his beer and looked over at me. "That's the four-million-dollar question," he said.

25

Lyel and I ate a burger at the Silver Dollar. When I returned home to the cabin, there was a single message on my answering machine. It was from Alicia: "Chris . . . I need help. I think something's happened to my father, and I can't call the police. I don't want to stay here. I'll wait for you at the Sawtooth Club until closing. Please come!"

The Sawtooth Club is a low-ceilinged bar and restaurant on Snow Lake's main street. Ski posters, a cozy sofa on either side of a central fireplace that separates the boozers from the diners. An episode of *The Twilight Zone* played on the bar television.

"Thank God," Alicia said. She was sitting at a table, a drink in front of her. Her concern was almost palpable. "I wanted to be someplace public, someplace I'd feel safe." I sat down across from her, with a view of the bar behind her.

"Alicia," I said as the waitress approached. I waved her off. "Talk to me."

"I confronted him. My dad. The name . . . you were right about that. I *did* recognize a name. When Dad was a kid, really young, five or six maybe, a friend of his, his best friend, was killed in a traffic accident. Johnny Crispell. When he was teaching me to drive he always used to mention Johnny Crispell, and how important it was to drive defensively, because you never knew who was in the other lane, never knew what was coming at you. I *knew* that name. And there it was on the board of trustees of Alpha Investments, and I knew that somehow Dad was involved in the warehouse thing. I knew he was into electronics, but I didn't know it was gray market and all of that." She paused. "I confronted him." Another pause. "He said he put Johnny's name on there as a remembrance to an old friend. He didn't think I'd remember the name, didn't think there was any way you would ever get that far—*we* would get that far—that I would ever see it. He screwed it up. Nothing new for him, I'm afraid. He's a grass-is-always-greener man, always has another deal that's going to work out big. He's a dreamer. I love him for it. He's managed to provide well for me, very well. Until now . . .

"When you mentioned the airport, and that a girl had died . . . well, I had overheard a couple calls about the airport. I knew he had some sort of interest in it. Something cooking. I told him you thought the girl's death had something to do with him. At first he denied it. He became furious with me. Then he broke down and cried." She wasn't looking at me. She sipped her drink. "I've seen my father do a lot of things, but I've never, ever, seen him cry. Not since Mom, anyway. And that was a long time ago."

I am not often at a loss for words, but I couldn't think of anything to say. It was sure to sound trite and insincere.

"He didn't have anything to do with the McGreggor girl, Chris, but he knew who did, and he admitted he had looked the other way. He told me he would make it right by me. Damn it," she said, wiping her sudden tears with a napkin, embarrassed. "Look at me! I'm a basket case." She took a deep breath. "He said he was going to call off the deal he had going and make the persons responsible turn themselves in," she began again, her voice only slightly unsteady. "He said that if they wouldn't, then he'd do it for them." After another taste of the drink she said, "He saw a quick buck and he tried to grab it. Didn't even explain to me what it was or how it worked, but he said some heads would roll, that he had let me down . . . let himself down, and he intended to fix it. Then he stormed out of the house, got in the car, and drove off. And he didn't come back. Left about three this afternoon and he didn't come back." Her tears began again.

"It hasn't been that long. There's no reason to think anything's happened."

She shook her head. "There *is*. I got this phone call right before I came over here. 'Alicia?' this weird voice says. 'Your father asked me to call you and say he's on his way home and that he wants you to stay there and wait for him.' Too strange for me, I'll tell you that. Why didn't Dad call if it was so important? So I took off. Got here and called you."

My mind was working quickly. I was glad I had Lyel parked across the street in his Wagoneer, keeping an eye on the place. It pays to have backup. My mistake was that I had parked right outside the Sawtooth Club, and my pickup truck is immediately recognizable. If Gebhardt had attempted to call things off, then my name had certainly come up, and if he had not returned, then his partner or partners were closing loopholes—and both Alicia and I were certainly loopholes. Lyel had a cellular phone in his Wagoneer, and rather than leave the building, I decided to try calling him from the pay phone.

The bar swarmed with people. A jazz duo was setting up in the far corner. I was beginning to feel claustrophobic. "I'm going to make a phone call. Why don't you come with me?"

"I'll make a rest stop, if you don't mind. Meet me back here."

I was tempted to follow her to the rest room and wait by the door; I had that sense of impending doom. But I wanted Lyel to position himself so that I could get Alicia out to the truck safely and to stay behind us as I drove her to the airport. And I wanted to do this quickly. I thought it ironic that the quickest means of escape would be the airport. If Gebhardt had mentioned his daughter to his partners, then she was at risk. I thought I could handle myself, especially if my opposition was the two deadbrains I had encountered in the hangar, the two who had sliced my ear. I owed them, and I actually looked forward to the opportunity to pay them back. I had come well armed. I carried my Detonics automatic and a couple of hidden razor blades. Lyel, too, had a concealed weapon on him. But having Alicia in tow complicated matters. I didn't like the idea of excess baggage. The best thing to do was either get her into Norton's custody or get her out of town. Both required a drive to Butte Peak, and I knew she wouldn't favor the idea of dealing with the police. I sensed she still hoped things could be resolved without their involvement. It was impossible, but the last thing I wanted to do was try and talk reason with her at that point.

So it meant a drive to Butte Peak. I wanted Lyel behind me. Lyel, with his cellular phone, could call in reinforcements if necessary. I headed to the pay phone in a coatrack alcove by the front entrance and placed the call. It rang twice. "Come on, Lyel," I urged. I looked out the window, but it was too dark to see if he was across the street.

What I did see, as I glanced back to look for Alicia, was Slim.

I was tall enough to see over the heads of the crowd. He came in the back door of the club, squeezed past the salad bar, and literally bumped into Alicia as she came

out of the ladies' room. At the same moment, a cowboy
at the bar bumped into a woman and knocked her drink
all over her. I could see the whole thing happen but was
helpless to do anything about it. The woman's boyfriend
had some words with the cowboy, and a fight broke out.
I dropped the phone and shoved my way to the pack.

Slim had Alicia; he was looking around for me—I assumed—but didn't see me. He must have been holding
a knife on her, for she cooperated fully, going ahead of
him toward the back door.

The fight separated us. The two men were on their
feet, wrestling. The bartender jumped the bar and tried
to intervene. I pushed harder, but the crowd had knotted into a tangled circle. Shoving matches were breaking out among the onlookers. I hesitated only briefly
before charging right into the thick of it. I was a full
head taller than anyone nearby and as wide as either
the cowboy or his opposition. I rudely pulled a few
onlookers out of my way and then charged the two
fighters, knocking both of them to the floor. A few
cheers went up. The fight stopped; both fighters had
been hurt going down. I blew through the other side of
the tight ring of fans that had formed around the fight
just as the back door shut behind Slim and Alicia.

My mistake was that I was in too big a hurry.

I slammed the back door's panic bar and burst out
into the narrow alley that led to a small parking lot for
the Magic Lantern movie theater. Slim and Alicia were
gone.

Someone else was behind me.

He sprang at me, delivered a devastating blow to my
lower back, and effortlessly caught my arm as I reached
for the Detonics holstered at my belt. Twisting my arm
painfully behind me, wrenching my elbow and shoulder, he removed my gun and marched me forward to a
waiting van not twenty feet away.

I didn't even get a look at the guy until I was in the

van. He had a big head, a thick neck, and narrow, deep-set eyes. The dead stare indicated an IQ right around room temperature. They had been lying in wait for me —expecting me to follow Slim and Alicia—and it made me furious that I was so predictable.

I cooperated only because I expected Lyel to appear and help out. When I realized that wasn't going to happen, and when I spotted a length of chain and two car batteries in the back of the van, I felt the heat of panic rush up my spine.

Big Head checked the chamber of my gun with his finger, never taking his eyes off me. That alone was disturbing: it meant he knew how to handle the thing. He slid the van's door shut, also without breaking eye contact, and the driver started the van.

We pulled away. When the man behind the wheel spoke, I recognized the voice as belonging to the logger type who had cut my ear. "Put the gun away, Danny," he said, as if scolding a dog. "We talked about how we're going to do this. Right?" Big Head nodded. "Pass it up here," Logger said. Big Head obeyed.

"Hands at your side," Big Head said slowly. "Face against the metal." I did as he said.

"Out for a little moonlight drive, are we?" I asked.

"You're making a lot of people nervous," Logger said, taking the turn a little fast. Big Head briefly lost his balance. The van swung to the left, and I guessed they were taking me to what in the winter was the bottom of Snow Lake's River Run ski lift. It was certainly remote enough, a half mile from anything, a giant open parking lot. A nice place to work a person over and then kill him.

One of the razor blades I had brought along was taped to the inside of my belt near the buckle, the other taped inside the belt at my back. People tend to tie you up with your hands either behind your back or in front of you. It pays to have a razor blade handy. As we turned, I moved my arm just enough to reach the blade in front. I could have performed some rather indelicate surgery with only minimal effort, but I waited. If they were smart, they would move me out of the van so that none of my blood was spilled in it and I couldn't be connected to them postmortem. That would be my best opportunity, I concluded. Furthermore, Lyel figured heavily in my chances of escape. I wanted to give him time to move in.

I said loudly, "Killing me won't rid Cousin of his problems," hoping to provoke a response.

Nothing.

Logger said, "You think too much." He tripped the car's tape system. Suddenly there was Pavarotti singing Schubert's "Ave Maria" in his rich tenor. A more incongruous backdrop for what they had planned I could not imagine: through the van's windows, the spectacular moonlit mountains, the glow of the small town's lights pinking the dark sky; all around me the incomparable sonorous tones of the great master. At the back of the van, two car batteries and a heavy chain.

I worried. Pavarotti was intended to cover my cries for help, providing Big Head didn't just snap my spine and get it over with.

"Where's Slim?" I asked.

Big Head countered with a kidney punch. The razor blade remained pinched between my sweaty fingers. The van slowed and bumped over the small bridge leading to the base hut of the ski lift.

We bounced to a stop and Logger killed the engine, cutting off Pavarotti in mid-syllable. The singer then returned to life as Logger twisted the key, engaging the battery and the stereo system with it. My bowels stirred. I am not a big fan of torture, especially my own. Logger climbed into the back with us and went to work organizing the two batteries and the jumper cables.

"We can skip this formality," he said, picking up the

jumper cables. "What do you have, as far as evidence, and where is it?"

"Evidence?" I said in my most naive tone.

"Klick, you're a stupid motherfucker. This shit is painful." He held up the toothed jaw of one of the jumper cable clamps, pulling a group of plastic binders out of his pocket. The binders are the industrial equivalent of garbage bag ties: a stem of the stiff plastic band slips through an opening in the other end; teeth prevent slippage.

Logger began working with the tow chains, and I had the complete picture firmly in mind. They would bind my wrists, chain my legs, and attempt to jump start me. If things became particularly nasty, they might even try jump starting my private parts, as Slim had threatened before—something I was even less anxious to experience. Lyel or not, I had to move now, before my hands were bound.

The mistake Logger made was to toss the plastic binders to Big Head. Conditioning demands we catch whatever is tossed to us. There was no real reason for him to catch the binders—Big Head could have just gone on working on me—but conditioning is stronger than thought, and his concentration was briefly broken as he reached out to attempt an awkward catch.

I spun quickly with the razor and slashed him from his shoulder to the opposite hip. It wasn't a deep cut, but it caused enough pain to drive him backward and into a stunned silence as he stared at the red streak across his shirt.

I had allowed Logger too much time to react, my attention fixed on Big Head. A blinding pulse of direct current zapped through me as Logger stabbed me with the twin copper jaws of the jumper cable. Every muscle in my body spasmed.

Clasping the rubber insulators, he leaned his weight

fully into me. My vision went red, and then there was
nothing. . . .

* * *

When I awakened, I was lying on the van's floor, my
hands bound by the plastic binders to the frame that
held the driver's seat, each ankle chained by means of a
tow hook to the oversize screw eyes usually used to
fasten down cargo. I wasn't going anywhere. Logger
had done a good job on me. I heard Big Head complaining in a childlike whine from the front seat. "It's no
good, I'm telling you. Look at all the blood! No fucking
way. I gotta get to a doctor," he said. "Now! You gotta
drive me. Or I'll drive myself. Give me the fucking
keys." In the resulting silence I could feel them both
looking at me. I was the problem.

"We kill the motherfucker," was Big Head's solution.
"Kill him and dump him and we'll take care of it later. I
gotta get my ass to a doctor. Now! I ain't waiting around
for no question-and-answer period."

"We're not going to kill him," Logger said.

"You afraid to kill the motherfucker? Hey, I'll kill the
bastard, no problem. I'll stomp his fucking brains in and
that'll be that. Give me a minute alone with him. It
won't take long."

At that moment I felt the van wiggle ever so slightly,
and relief flooded through me. I immediately began
writhing on the floor, willing to give away the fact that I
was no longer unconscious, in my attempt to disguise
the fact that Lyel was finally with us. I hoped the mild
shaking meant he was blocking the exhaust pipe, which
would mean the van wouldn't start. There was no way
to tell how much he knew about what was going on
inside, but the thing about Lyel is that he fights with his
head; five of these guys would have had a rough time

going up against him once he developed a plan, and I
sensed he had already worked one out.

"Ah fuck, man. I gotta get me to the hospital fast.
Look at this! Christ, I'm losing pints here." The sudden
heavy silence had a unique, familiar intensity to it. I
knew prior to the dull and hollow cap-gun pop that Big
Head was facing a weapon. The flat sound died inside
the van faster than Big Head did. I heard him twitch in
his seat a few times—there is no uglier sound—and then
he went still.

"Couldn't have him going to the hospital like that,"
Logger said calmly, still holding the weapon, a Heckler
& Koch P7M13 double-action semiautomatic, an im-
pressive combat handgun, as he stepped over me into
the back of the van. I didn't know what he had done
with my Detonics. He clamped the ground cable to the
chain, smiling strangely. It is a well-documented fact
that a peculiar switch is thrown in any man after a
human kill, and that in some the effect is that killing
becomes easier, almost addictive. Logger had the glassy
eyes of a drinker; he was suddenly high and excited,
showing no remorse whatsoever. Out of control. I had
been uncertain earlier; now I knew that this man could
and would kill.

One advantage a potential victim of this physiological
high has is that the killer becomes overconfident. Criminals have been known to confess their crimes in this
heightened state: believing themselves superior, they
are often anxious to display this superiority by claiming
bragging rites.

I was helpless. I needed to slow Logger down and
distract him in order to give Lyel more time; I had to
fuel his sense of control over me in the hope that his
overconfidence might provide me an opening, although
at that moment I couldn't think what that opening
might be.

"Is that how you did in Bert McGreggor?" I asked.

"With a gun? Or was she in the car when you blew it up?" His breathing was fast and furious. In the dim light inside the van, the huge man kneeling at my feet, the gun in one hand, a jumper cable in the other, was a terrifying sight. I tried to sound casual. It was an effort. "You're going to kill me anyway."

"You, I can't put a bullet through. Cause too much of a hassle. Danny, what the shit do I care?" Had he even heard me?

"You'll have to get rid of the body," I reminded him.

"In my line of work, that's not a problem," he said.

It wasn't a good time for my brain to malfunction, but I couldn't think of anything to say.

"Here's the thing, Klick," he said, putting down his weapon and picking up the other jumper cable—if I survived this, it would be a long time before I ever jump-started a car again. "You have some evidence. We know you do. The girl told her father; the father told us. I need to know what it is and where it is. Then I need to find it and destroy it. Now that I've killed Daniel in front of you, as you just pointed out, it's no longer a question of whether I kill you, but when I kill you. A reasonable man would want the last two hours of his life to be at least somewhat enjoyable. I can't offer that. But I can offer to keep them free of pain. And if you think this is pain," he said, lifting my pants leg and touching the claws of the jumper cables to my shinbone, "then you don't know much." He was grinning.

Each time he did that, my system seemed to stop completely. I didn't feel my heartbeat; I certainly didn't breathe. And then suddenly there was a freight train in my chest, timpani in my ears, and a splitting headache tearing at my temples. I felt my eyes water and the teardrops run down my cheeks. My nose congested. I had a hard-on.

"Where can I find this evidence, Klick, or were you

bullshitting?" He paused. "You strike me as a big bull-shitter."

I felt the van rock again. In one defeating instant I realized that it had not been Lyel outside the van, but only the wind. I was alone.

With this realization came absolute panic; I couldn't seem to get my breath, and my mind reeled with distasteful images. He leaned over my feet to zap me again. In panic, I raised my hips, stretching myself, using what little slack there was in the tow chains, and brought the toe of my right shoe under his chin as if I was kicking open a trap door. His head went straight back with a snap, and I heard his teeth clap shut. He catapulted backward, collapsing in shock and pain. I shook my leg furiously, trying to disconnect the chain's hook from the screw eye in the floor.

I heard him moan—I couldn't see him from where I lay. I had failed to knock him out. There was only one thing at that moment that I feared more than this man, and that was this man in a full-blown rage.

The gun was only inches from my left foot. I couldn't reach it. I continued to shake the chain, hoping to unhook it.

It was Logger who undid it for me. He shook off the effects of my kick, and in his hurry to hurt me, he reached out and grabbed the chain just as I gave it a good firm kick. The hook came loose from the screw eye.

I kicked the heavy chain toward my head and then jerked my leg forward, delivering the chain straight at him like a bullwhip. The big man raised his hand to block it. It struck his forearm and he nearly got hold of it, but I jerked back, stealing it from him. The hook caught him in the face. He got to his knees, looking to me as frightening as a bear rearing on its hind legs. His nose was bleeding.

A fraction of an instant of time had become an eon to

me. I had time to think. I saw him coming at me; I saw the fallen jumper cable lying within reach of my leg. I knew damn well how hot it was. And I thought I knew better than he. I was somewhat conditioned to the current; he was not.

Again, I whipped the chain at him. Again, I saw him reach out to block it, to grab it, to stop me. But this time I lowered my bare leg to the jumper cable. This time we would both fry.

The chain coiled around his waist. As I brought my leg down onto the cable's copper jaw and felt the current stinging through me, I faintly saw his eyes light up in horror. I screamed loudly in an attempt to overcome the pain, to outlast him. He screamed out of agony and terror.

We stayed like this for what felt like several minutes. It couldn't have been more than a few seconds. The volume of our release was deafening in the small enclosure. Our eyes met, and I felt my lip twitch into a curled, tortured smile of defiance. I would outlast him. His eyes rolled and he keeled over backward. I jerked my burned leg from the cable.

With one leg already free I was able to unhook my right leg as well. Then I struggled up into a sitting position so that my bound hands were at my lower back. It took me several minutes—it seemed like _hours_—to wrestle myself into a position where I could get hold of the second razor blade and cut myself free.

I was free.

I then used the leftover plastic ties to secure my captor, binding his ankles and wrists. His wallet told me he was Kevin Hale. I dumped Big Head in the back with Hale, recovered both guns, and drove away.

Pavarotti had never sounded so sweet.

26

I drove the van into town and called Lyel's cellular car phone from the Chevron station's pay phone. He answered on the first ring.

"It's me," I said, a slight tremor in my voice.

"He's got Alicia in an old miner's camp down here on Broadmore. Couple of shacks down here," Lyel said softly. "What the hell took you so long?"

"Me? You were supposed to back up me! Where the hell were *you*?"

"Priorities," he said. "Ladies first. What's your situation?"

"One dead, one under restraint." I told him. "He blew away his own man."

"We need to get Alicia away from him. I hate to say this, but I think the cops will only make a mess of things. This needs to be handled delicately, and I just don't see them doing that."

"Agreed."

"How soon can you get here?" he asked.

"I'm on my way."

Twenty-five minutes later I parked the van next to his Wagoneer in a copse of cottonwoods. I was somewhat familiar with this area of Broadmore Road, as was he; his house and the guest cottage were only a few miles away.

This land was part of a four-hundred-acre parcel that ran north from the old mine to the big bend in the river. Clarence Stilwill, a mutual friend, rented a log home close by.

I joined Lyel in the Wagoneer. The odors in that van were horrible.

"Any action?"

"No. Nothing."

"Perhaps Slim is awaiting the arrival of Hale and his dead friend," I said. "We have their van; we could take it in and hope he thinks they're driving up."

"Too risky," he said. "What if he's *not* expecting them?"

"Agreed."

Lyel looked at me. "So what do we do?"

"We have Kevin. Kevin's done some very bad things, but from what I saw in the hangar that night, it's Slim who gives the orders. If Kevin talked, Slim would have problems. We could suggest a trade."

"We could indeed. But why did Slim take Alicia?"

"To pressure Gebhardt. He apparently wasn't involved in the killings. When his daughter confronted him, he decided to step out of the deal."

"So Alicia is their leverage," he said.

"Yes."

"Which means they'll need to convince Gebhardt they have her."

"True," I agreed.

"So will they bring him out here to prove it? Because if they will, that might give us an opening."

"Good point," I said.

He glanced over his shoulder at the van, parked slightly behind us.

"There's just one problem," Lyel said.

"What's that?"

"You didn't leave the side door to the van open, did you?"

27

It appeared that the killer Kevin Hale had found one of my razor blades and cut himself free. In my haste, I had forgotten about the first razor, the one I'd used to slice Big Head. It was critical he not reach Slim in the old miner's camp before we could get there.

Lyel understood this instinctively. We quickly discussed our options and decided he would head straightaway toward the camp and its cabins, while I circled along the river, which from the first few tracks we encountered, seemed to be the direction Hale had headed. I kept my Detonics. He took the Heckler & Koch. What I didn't tell Lyel was that I had failed to search the van thoroughly for any other weapons. For all I knew, Hale was carrying.

Next to the van I noticed a small creased piece of white paper. I picked it up and thought I recognized what it was. I touched my tongue delicately to it; Lyel gave me a puzzled expression.

"Cocaine," I said quickly. "That won't help us any."

Lyel and I split up: he headed off through the woods in a straight line for the miners camp. I cut over toward the river, pausing behind a cottonwood here, crouching behind the undergrowth there, all the while listening for his movement ahead. I kept in mind that he was coked up, possibly unaware of pain, artificially alert for the smallest of sounds, unpredictable.

I knew the river snaked in a big S before heading past the camp so I cut a path through the woods to the first major turn in the river as a shortcut.

I first noticed him as I approached this larger bend. Caught in the stark moonlight, he was moving quickly along the river's edge. It was almost like looking through one-way glass, in that he certainly could not see me within the darkness of the cottonwoods, yet I was allowed an occasional glimpse of him as he stole along at a brisk pace. Even at this distance, the sight of him brought a chill. He moved with a jerky, tense gait.

Surprise was my only ally, if one discounted Lyel. Lyel's present responsibility was containment. Mine was pursuit. If I hurried, I could cut my quarry off.

As the spring thaw delivers snow melt in volumes too great for the river to handle, the riverbed swells. Its banks decay like glaciers calving, and the river, year by year, changes course, leaving behind a ragged devastation of the vegetation along its banks, from the smallest blade of grass to the biggest tree. As a result, the banks of the Middle Wood River are blanketed annually with huge fallen cottonwood trees, which often congregate, forming log jams at bends in the river. These jams force the water to flow around them, forming a new channel for the river and causing further erosion, more destruction of the environs. One byproduct of this bank deterioration is dead trees scattered along the river's edge. And fallen trees make great cover.

I reached the bend first, my attention fixed on Kevin Hale, who moved toward me quickly.

Time was working against me. Any second he might glance in my direction, and I would be fully exposed. One hope was that in the moonlight he might miss me completely were I to remain still. But better than that, I favored distraction. I resorted to an age-old ruse: I flung a river rock well beyond him and to his left, deep into the woods, where it shattered the quiet night with a crash of twigs and branches. I could imagine what that would do to a coked-up brain. Kevin Hale stopped short and raised a gun.

Spotting the gun, I hesitated. Gunfire would alert Slim and spoil the chances of luring him into a vulnerable situation.

I could allow Hale to pass by and reach the cabins, but that was an even worse option.

I launched a second rock into the woods; it made a sound like a person stumbling through the brush. Kevin Hale dropped to one knee, ready now to fire.

Then came the glance over the shoulder as his reeling brain figured it out. Or perhaps he had heard me. We were staring at each other across a moonlit expanse of river shore, no more than twenty feet separating us. I charged him at a full run.

For me, those twenty feet closed in slow motion: step . . . step . . . step . . . Hale pivoted, lost his footing on the rock, and reached out to catch himself . . . ten feet . . . he swung the gun around until it was aimed directly at me. I dived . . .

He never got off the shot.

I landed on him with my full weight. His head twisted badly, and something in his neck cracked, and as he turned to look at me with those eerie, glassy eyes of his, he grinned.

I knocked the gun, a .38 revolver, from his grasp and kneed him in the chest, hoping to knock the wind out of him. But the blow had no effect. He didn't seem to feel it.

"Asshole," he said, and lifted me off him as if I were a mannequin. That's when I suspected that it wasn't cocaine but PCP, the superhuman drug. My tongue was not well-trained. I might as well have been wrestling a

gorilla, it made him that strong. He dumped me onto
the rocks.

Seeing him in the moonlight, with his skin a disquiet-
ing shade of gray-blue, his neck wrenched horribly to
one side, and his eyes drug-crazed and unfocused, for a
fleeting moment I wondered if Kevin Hale could be
beaten. I didn't like the odds.

I kicked him in the shin, jumped to my feet, and
drove both hands up under his jaw, throwing him backward. I heard his head hit a rock as he landed—and yet
he got up, quickly. He tried to knee me again, but this
time I danced to the side, taking instead a strong left to
the ear. A loud *whomp* filled my head, and he struck me
again before I drew back my arm and delivered my fist
into the very center of his face, obliterating his nose.
Again he went down, but he wasn't finished.

I had broken some bones in my hand with the punch;
it hurt like hell. I had no desire to use it again.

But I had to.

He came at me wildly. If not broken, his neck was
certainly dislocated. How could this *thing* still be moving, much less fighting? Where his nose had been, there
was mashed flesh; blood smeared his beard. He tackled
me, crushing me under his weight as we went down.

We both reached for rocks at the same time.

I lifted my left arm as a shield, blocked his effort, and
hammered a good-size stone into the side of his head. It
made a ghastly sound.

He dropped his rock and fell off me, unconscious.

Finally.

Lyel appeared from within the woods. "Jesus!" he
hissed strongly at the sight of the man.

"Imbalanced blood chemistry," I said.

We used Hale's shoelaces to bind his hands and feet.
Lyel tore off the man's shirt sleeve, and used it to gag
him.

"We could toss him in the river and drown him," I suggested.

"Wouldn't want to pollute it," Lyel said. "Slim's vehicle isn't working any longer," he informed me. "He's having coil problems."

We moved on down the rocky river shore and ducked into the woods along the game trail Lyel had used to reach the river. It was only a matter of minutes before we cleared the woods, crested the knoll, and ducked behind an outcropping of rock that overlooked the group of dilapidated cabins below. A dim yellow light, battery powered no doubt, glowed in one.

"What now?" I whispered.

Typically, Lyel already had it worked out.

* * *

We split up on top of the ridge. Because of my exhaustion, bruises, and broken bones, Lyel made me take the more passive role of heading to Slim's truck while he stole quietly down the side of the hill and worked his way to the back wall of the far cabin. I held the Detonics tightly in my right hand, safety off, barrel pointed carefully at the ground, away from my body. I reached Slim's truck and waited for Lyel to get into position.

The truck was unlocked, keys in the ignition. I popped the door open, and slid my thumb into the jamb to trip the button that controlled the dome light. It flashed briefly. I then reached around the steering column, delicately rotated the key a notch until the dash lights flashed, and hit the horn twice before slipping back out and easing the door closed, eyes straining through the truck's windows to watch the door of the far cabin.

It took him a few seconds. The light inside the cabin went dead. The door finally opened slowly and I saw his thin, wiry form. He was staring out at his truck, staring in my direction, and I had to wonder what was going through his head. Would he take Alicia with him as cover, or would he not even bother to investigate? Lyel had waved from the far corner, and I could only pray that this would work. A person's curiosity is much more dependable and stable than a person's anger. To confront Slim might mean putting Alicia in even greater jeopardy than she was in already. The idea was to tease him out, hope he came without her, and deal with him efficiently.

"In here," Slim yelled from the doorway.

We had problems.

Slim had expected Kevin Hale after all. With so many cabins to choose from, he must have thought that Kevin couldn't locate him, hence his invitation. Unfortunately, he was not amateurish enough to be drawn into the open. We had underestimated both him and the situation, and now we would be forced, one way or the other, to show our hand: if I stepped out from behind the truck into the moonlight, he would see clearly that I was not Kevin Hale; if I didn't respond soon, he would be alerted to our scam and possibly harm Alicia.

Lyel sensed this. I watched him spin out of sight, heading back around the cabin, and I knew he expected me to do what had to be done: to aim for the heart, to fire without warning.

I froze.

I couldn't do it. I had both hands on my Detonics, the hammer drawn back, but I could not raise my arms for all the strength in me. One shot was all I had to squeeze out. One shot at that darkness in the open cabin door. One unannounced shot aimed at his heart. But it was not to be. Not from me.

The door was flung open, nearly torn off its old hinges, and he had her gripped by that beautiful hair, a weapon at her back. Her blouse was torn open, a breast partially exposed. Suddenly there it was, the very rage I had not been able to summon. Now, but for her presence, I could have emptied nine shots into him. But she stood between him and me, and he walked carefully ahead, checking over his shoulder repeatedly, stealing any chance Lyel might have to sneak up on him.

"Who's there?" he called out, coming closer.

I don't like to think of myself as one who panics, but the adrenaline that pumped into my veins with the sight of her sent improper signals to my brain, erasing the slate. Blank. Ten yards off now and closing, still checking over his shoulder expertly.

I crouched down further. Slim and Alicia were fifteen feet from the truck. *Think*, damn it! Where the hell had my reasoning gone?

"Looking for me?" I heard Lyel ask from the cabin. Slim stopped and turned. "Hey, what the hell, mister? You all right, lady?" Lyel added naively, as if he had just happened to stumble onto this cabin in the wee hours of the morning. I used the distraction to inch my way forward. Slim released her arms. He had a knife at her spine, but they were still too close together to risk a shot.

"Hey, what the hell, friend? Can't a guy and his woman find a little privacy?"

"You all right, lady?" Lyel repeated.

The knife rubbed across the back of her blouse. "A little embarrassed," she said in a wonderfully controlled voice. She knew Lyel, of course, and it must have been a tremendous relief to see his face, even at a distance. Hope. It brought her to a point of momentary control.

Lyel shouted, "I patrol this here property, *friend,* and I seen your headlights coming in a while ago, and I hate to tell you this, but I got no problem if you and your little lady want some privacy, but it'll have to be somewhere else, I'm afraid. This here is a staked claim, and you're trespassing, and I'm afraid I got to ask you to leave. I'm carrying, *friend.* We get some kids in here from time to time want to prove they're hung like stallions. A couple shots usually scare them off just fine. I seen your truck, I honked the horn and hid in case you were some deadbrain kid doing drugs and figuring on shootin' my ass. Now, I got no problem with nothing if you and your lady friend there want to pack it up and move it. But you give me trouble, *friend,* and you're going to get it back. We got that straight?"

"No problem," Slim said. Lyel had all his attention. I straightened.

"I've got no problem with that," he said again. "What's between the woman and me is my business, thanks just the same."

"I don't think so," I said loudly, my gun in low-ready. His arm drew back to stab her.

The sound of my voice scared Alicia. She jumped, tearing loose from his hold. I brought the gun up smoothly and quickly, aimed for the heart, and squeezed off a round. He flew backward in a spray of blood, issuing an agonized cry I will never forget. He landed heavily, a frightening finality to his fall. Alicia saw his wound and vomited.

Lyel kicked the stiletto from Slim's hand and bent to feel the man's neck for a pulse. He looked up at me.

I felt strangely on the edge of tears. I had killed a man. I could have rushed him . . . I could have left it to Lyel . . . I could have . . .

"He's alive," Lyel said.

28

Sheriff Norton met us at the hospital. He spoke to the doctors, talked briefly to both the men we had brought in, and then joined Lyel and me in the waiting room. Alicia was under sedation, soon to be sleeping soundly in room 111.

"You all right?" Norton asked, pointing to the bandage on the back of my leg. The third finger of my right hand was splinted. It felt too tender to mess with.

"Burned myself," I explained. "Had a little run-in with a pair of Diehards—the twelve-volt variety. Kevin Hale introduced me to shock therapy. I returned the favor."

"One dead, one shot, one beat to a pulp. You're going to spend the next six months in court, you know that, don't you?"

"I had a feeling I would be needing an attorney," I said.

"That's an understatement." He produced a Ziploc plastic bag and held it open for me. "I'd appreciate it if you would deposit your weapon in here," he said.

"I think that may be a little premature," I said. "This isn't over yet."

"For you it is."

I shook my head. "I realize you can lock me up. But if you do, I—we—won't tell you anything."

"I wasn't going to, but if you keep talking that way, I just might change my mind," Norton said.

"No sense in the three of us getting in each other's way."

"There's something else," Lyel said, breaking his silence.

"What's what?" Norton asked.

"There are political overtones to all of this, and the evidence isn't exactly all there. It involves Brandon Cousin. And there may or may not be a hostage situation. You'll need a warrant for Cousin, or at least probable cause. We," he said, looking at me, "on the other hand, do not."

"You do or do not have evidence?" Norton asked angrily.

I said, "We have lots of evidence, but most of it is circumstantial. We have the blackmail money and the legal description of the land in Bert's handwriting. We have Cousin's name and Corwin's, also in her handwriting. We have proof that several corporations have dummy boards of directors. There may be fingerprints on that cash, there may be a money trail back to Gebhardt. If we find Corwin, he may talk."

"He's our best bet," Lyel added, "because he seems to have been in on this early. He'd make one hell of a state's witness. If he's alive."

"Or one of these two goons may talk, if they're offered a deal," I continued. "The point being, there *is* evidence. But it needs development. You can't cut a warrant on it, and we can't leave Gebhardt hanging out."

"The way I would do this if I were Cousin," Lyel said, "is to execute the deal immediately. He needs Gebhardt for that. The commission made their recommendation. Cousin keeps Gebhardt quiet for a day or two while the papers go through, a week or two if necessary.

There is one hell of a lot of money at stake here. Alicia was to be used to pressure Gebhardt. Once they had Alicia, they could have released Gebhardt and told him to stay in line until the deal went down. That miner's camp was just a holding tank until Klick here had been dealt with. Then they would have taken her out of town to a little farmhouse somewhere and sat on her until Gebhardt's dummy corporations sold the land and Gebhardt gave Cousin his cut. Then, of course, if they were shrewd, they would eventually kill both Gebhardt and his daughter."

"There's a good chance," I said, "that Gebhardt knew nothing of the killings. If that's true, he may be willing to testify against Cousin. The feds are after a gray-market deal he had going. If a plea bargain could be cut, I bet Gebhardt would sing. But all of this is moot if we don't find him and get him free."

Norton stared at me, looking a little perplexed. "You're saying I would have a hell of a time getting an arrest warrant, and an even more difficult time justifying an arrest without a warrant." He sighed. "You're probably right."

"And it's not exactly like Cousin's friends—and both our judges are chummy with the man—are going to be anxious to issue those warrants," Lyel pointed out. "They all ran on the same side of the ticket, don't forget."

"But," I said, "were Lyel and I to break in to Cousin's house—and that's where we'd start looking for Gebhardt—well, then. The Sheriff can arrive to bust *us*, not Cousin, and anything you happen to find in the process . . ."

Norton was nodding now. "I would have to bust you," he said.

"What are lawyers for?" Lyel said. "If Klick's going to be in court, I might as well be too."

"One of my patrols just happens to see you going inside," Norton said.

"Something like that," I agreed.

"That's conspiracy," Norton stated matter-of-factly.

"That's show biz," I said.

He held the plastic bag out again, shaking it. "I'll want that gun," he said.

"Understood."

Lyel added, "Just make sure to leave us alone in there long enough to get Cousin talking. You can add another charge to our sheet, Chief."

"What's that?" Norton asked.

"Theft. I'm going to borrow one of those," he said, pointing through a glass window at a row of five micro-cassette tape recorders that the doctors used for dictation.

"It's inadmissible," Norton said.

"It is if *you* carried the tape recorder. But a private citizen? The courts may be more lenient. It can't hurt, Dan. You need evidence? Maybe we can get you some evidence."

"I'll give you ten minutes in there with him. Then we're coming in after you. And remember: Cousin is the good guy. He's the citizen we're trying to protect."

"Understood."

"I hope so," said Norton, looking troubled. "I hope this isn't a big mistake." He was looking at me when he made that statement.

* * *

A quarter mile down the road from Cousin's house, Lyel killed the headlights and pulled the Wagoneer to the side of the road. The house reminded me of a Cape Cod beach house—a saltbox with a few contemporary touches like skylights and oversized windows.

I produced my pick kit and removed the three tools I thought I would need.

He said, "Lights are on. That's encouraging."

"It may mean they're expecting someone. Someone like Slim."

"That's discouraging."

"We'll cut around back and go in on that wooded side if we can."

"Agreed."

We stayed on the low side of a landscaping berm heavily planted in young aspen, edging along the Cousin property. Then we cut quickly across the lawn and slipped into shadow along the wall of the house. My nerves were on edge. The chorus of crickets and frogs sounded too loud, almost deafening—every sense was on high alert. Gun drawn, Lyel tried the doorknob. I was ready to step up and use my picking talents, but to our surprise, the door was unlocked.

Lyel stepped inside, gun extended out in front of him in low-ready. Our only light came from the partially opened door in front of us. We both observed and absorbed the floor plan. The kitchen was immediately to our left; I could hear the whine of the refrigerator. Oddly, the door in front of us, which stood open, led downstairs and into a basement. Lyel took a second to start the tape recorder running and then returned it to his top pocket. The choice was up or down, main floor or basement. I motioned for us to move through the kitchen, squeezed past Lyel and led the way.

It was a strange, frightening feeling to be creeping around someone else's house. We made it through the kitchen silently and without notice. Lyel pointed down the short hall that doubled as a wet bar. I nodded.

This led us into a very small dining room, and beyond that we heard voices. We crossed the dining room carefully, but could go no farther without being seen.

Lyel risked it and peered carefully around the corner.

He leaned back toward me and held up three fingers, and then shook his head: three people, no Gebhardt. The conversation was one of mumbles and difficult to interpret; it was as if they were speaking a foreign language. I shrugged and pointed down toward the basement. Did he want to try that first? He shook his head no, removed the tape recorder, and slid the machine carefully around the corner to where its condenser microphone would have a good ear on the conversation. We waited patiently for what felt like five minutes—but was probably more like two—letting the tape recorder run, hoping we were getting something of interest.

I was growing impatient when I heard the distinct sound of a gun being cocked behind us.

"Not even so much as a twitch, gentlemen." He made Lyel drop the gun. "Keep both hands where I can see them," he added, removing the gun from Lyel's hand.

We turned slowly. "Lyel," I said. "I'd like you to meet Jason Hanright. Mr. Hanright is the attorney from San Francisco I told you so much about. Mr. Hanright has power of attorney for Pacific Rim Leasing."

Cousin came around the corner, looked at me, and shook his head. "What a dumb shit you are," he said.

Hanright marched us into the living room like a bad scene from an old Cagney movie, hands on our heads. There were three of them, as Lyel had indicated: Cousin, a woman old enough to be his wife, and a worried man in his mid-fifties. We were patted down by the worried man. I thought I knew who he was. "James Corwin, if I'm not mistaken."

"The trouble with you, Klick," said Cousin in an angry voice, "is that you rarely are mistaken." I was reminded of Steven Garman's comment about Cousin swinging a big stick when he wanted to, this wasn't a man one wanted to cross. I was a little late in that assessment.

"Norton is right behind us," Lyel said.

Cousin smiled, not buying it. "Good. Then he can arrest you and save us the trouble of making the phone call. Or did I miss something? Is it illegal to have some friends over to your house for a drink?"

"Depends what you've done with Gebhardt," I said. "We think he's here. We were *told* he's here. If he *is,* then I'd say you have big problems."

"Big*ger* problems," Lyel corrected. "Alicia Gebhardt is in police protection as we speak. Kidnapping charges have been filed against your henchmen, and they've brought your name into things, Mr. Cousin."

Cousin replied confidently, "If that were the case, Dan Norton would be here himself. Wouldn't he?"

Cousin struck me as a man overly proud of his own planning. I said, "You closed the highway on the day of the 'accident' you staged. That was *your* mistake, Cousin. It's too much of a coincidence. It tipped your hand." I faced the other man. "And yours, Mr. Corwin," I said, "was underestimating Roberta McGreggor. You know you're an accomplice to murder, don't you?"

"Two murders and a kidnapping," Lyel corrected. "Two kidnappings. Not to mention extortion, forgery, and a host of other charges."

"We can handle this," Cousin assured Corwin in his thick country twang.

"Like you handled the McGreggors?" I asked.

"It's over," said Corwin. "What's the use?"

Hanright disagreed. "It's *far* from over. These men broke into your house, Brandon. I suggest *you* call the police."

"I was thinking of a plane ride," said Cousin. "A little jump to the desert floor for these two."

"Shut up, Brandon," warned Hanright. "They're guessing. There is no reason to jump to ugly conclusions. We have business to conduct. We mustn't overlook that fact."

Lyel stiffened. But I relaxed: the tape recorder would have caught Cousin's threat.

Hanright was a big, confident man—along with Cousin, the one to worry about. The weak link was Corwin. He clearly sensed that this was out of his control. He didn't strike me as a killer as much as a greedy assessor who had seen a fast buck.

"Business to conduct? Doing a little late-night paperwork, are we?" Lyel asked, stepping forward now to challenge Hanright. "Forcing Gebhardt to sign a few documents maybe. Shifting the blame while keeping the profits?"

"Wouldn't have anything to do with a section of land south of Timmerman Hill, would it?" I asked.

Corwin snapped his head to look at me. Defeat registered on his face.

I decided Hanright was not stupid enough to shoot us. I tested this out by saying, "You can shoot that thing if you want, but I'm going to find Mr. Gebhardt and have a discussion with him about turning all of you in. If you want to stop me, it will require shooting me in the back. And that's never been big with juries. After that, of course, you will have to shoot my friend Mr. Lyel. And then you will have to explain the gunshots to the Sheriff, who is parked outside just waiting for an excuse to come in here. And if you don't believe us, you can take a look."

Corwin rushed to the window.

"I think I'll join you," Lyel said.

"Don't," Hanright warned, stepping forward and waving the pistol at Lyel. Lyel grinned at him and continued walking.

"I don't see anyone," Corwin said anxiously from the window.

"Shred everything," the woman said. "They obviously know about the land deal. Brandon, shred it all!"

The *land deal:* sweet music. The tape recorder was still running.

Hanright didn't like it. He looked over at her, about to protest.

Lyel shoved him and we broke into a run. We rounded the corner into the kitchen, and then bounded downstairs.

The basement had been converted into a television room/study with a couple doors off a short hallway. Only one of the doors was locked. I kicked it in. Gebhardt stared back at me, pale and listless, from the corner sitting at a desk.

Footsteps pounded down the stairs.

There is something contagious about panic. Hanright charged Lyel. Cousin, a moment behind him, shook Lyel's handgun at me, indicating for me to move away from Gebhardt, which I did. Hanright didn't seem like a killer; Cousin I was less sure about. That was when I noticed the papers there, and the pen beside them. Gebhardt *was* being forced to sign something over to these two—Lyel had been right about that—and as of yet there was no signature.

Lyel tangled up with Hanright. I cut over to the desk. Cousin put a bullet into the ceiling as a warning, hitting a water pipe in the process. The ceiling started leaking. He glanced overhead.

The trick in such situations is to take advantage of any opening and move quickly, without thinking it over.

Cousin's eyes flinched up and I reacted. I swung my right leg—hurt knee and all—slightly to my left, then kicked straight out and up toward the man's left shoulder, catching the gun in the process.

He fired the weapon as my kick made contact.

Lyel reacted instantly, kicking into the side of Hanright's knee, cracking it loudly. Hanright cried out and went down in pain.

Cousin's bullet entered Anthony Gebhardt's chest

strongly enough to knock him and his chair over. Lyel grabbed the gun from behind. I kicked Cousin in the chest and sent him reeling into the wall. He slumped to the floor.

I hurried to Gebhardt's side. "It's bloody, but he'll live," I told Lyel, who was standing watch over Hanright and Cousin. Wisely, he had not picked up Cousin's gun, leaving Cousin's prints intact.

"Good thing, too," Lyel said without looking over, his attention still on the two fallen men, "because Anthony Gebhardt just became our star witness."

29

Two weeks later, Lyel and I were in our usual positions on the deck of the guest cabin. The sprinkler system was nearly finished; I had only to fill in the ditches and pack the soil. I was tired and I smelled like epoxy. I trained the binoculars on that hole in the cottonwood tree and studied the red-shafted flickers as they came and went. A rum and tonic waited patiently on the picnic table, half empty. Lyel held his in hand.

Derby slept between us, legs twitching in dreamland.

"You're upset," I said.

Lyel slurped and then said, "I'm upset that some deranged human being like Hale can confess to murdering two women, and then claim chemical dependency as a means of attempting to skate. I'm upset that the one who you call Slim can get sewn up in Salt Lake and can trade down a kidnapping charge to assault with a deadly weapon for information on Hale. But most of all I'm upset that greed could do this to people. My God, Klick, where does it stop?"

"It doesn't. They stood to make several million dollars. That kind of temptation is formidable. At least we can be thankful the Timmerman property will eventually be in the county's hands." The feds had seized it using racketeering laws.

"It's the principle of the thing," he complained.

"Lyel, you *have* that kind of money. Some of us don't."

We sat in silence then. I had offended him, and it hurt both of us.

"Well," he finally said, "since you've managed to ruin my day, allow me to ruin yours."

In the open ditches, the PVC sprinkler system looked like the long white bones of a prehistoric creature.

I knew who it was from before the postcard ever reached me. It had to do with the composition of the card: a single pink heart on a background of pale yellow. *Her.* I accepted it from Lyel, not flipping it over. He left me alone: he knew me well.

He said softly, "It was in the box." We shared a mailbox at the end of the dirt road.

It was addressed to both of us. That hurt me. Selfishly, I wanted her all to myself.

Miss you, it read. A little cloud drawn in ink with lightning bolts beneath it to remind me of that incredible night we had shared. *Don't forget me*, it finished. She signed it *Nicole*, not Nicky, I noted. That was one in my favor.

"I won't," I told the card, my throat tight. "I can't seem to," I added sadly.

I looked up. Lyel was gone.

Yes, he knew me well.

* * *

A few minutes later Lyel rounded the corner of the deck. Held in his big mitt of a hand was a brand-new Winston graphite rod with a Hardy reel. A gift for me. "Your shoulder can't take this yet, but I thought you would like to see it in action."

"Thanks," I said.

Lyel led the way to the slough. To Zeus. And Apollo.

Derby caught up to us in excitement. She stayed close by my side.

"I'd rather you didn't go," Lyel said, making the first cast.

I didn't say anything. I felt the breeze of autumn grace my cheeks. I saw Lyel deliver the fly perfectly, and the fish rise to the fly.